The Cats *that* Broke *the* Spell

Karen Anne Golden

Copyright

This book or eBook is a work of fiction. Names, characters, places and incidents are products of the author's imagination or are used fictitiously. Any resemblance to actual events, locales, persons or cats, living or dead, is entirely coincidental.

ISBN-13: 978-1544009131

ISBN-10: 1544009135

Overture

By the magic of my black cats,

This man holds me back.

Scarecrow, set things right.

Erie Witch Incantation

Table of Contents

Chapter One

Early-September

Katherine "Katz" Cokenberger, a twenty-nine-year-old heiress to millions, sat on a Victorian wingback chair and scanned the room for the locations of her seven cats. Three sat on the tall wood valances over the turret windows. Two were underneath her chair, pawing at the lining to either add or remove stolen items from their stash. And two were engaged in their early morning reconnaissance mission, exploring every nook and cranny of the seventeen-room, pink painted Victorian house.

She took a deep breath and let it out slowly, savoring the happy moment. She was thankful to be able to relax lately.

In the small town of Erie, Indiana, northwest of Indianapolis, seven months had gone by without a murder, arson, or kidnapping. The only home invasion reported in the *Erie Ledger* was by a family of raccoons that had broken into a house through the doggy door. Chief London had thrown up his hands and said he couldn't charge the

1

masked thieves because they ate the evidence. He had also said he couldn't arrest them because he didn't have handcuffs small enough to fit them. This was his running joke with Katherine about her cats. He knew two of them would steal anything they could sink their fangs into.

Katherine counted her personal blessings. First, there hadn't been a murder in the pink mansion since the dead of winter, when her childhood friend showed up with the Russian mob. Second, the mansion hadn't suffered any damage from water heater explosions, fires or tornadoes. Third, with the new security system at the mansion and with her best friend's mum living back in Manhattan, there hadn't been any home invasions. Last, there hadn't been a ghost sighting in either the mansion or the Foursquare next door.

To her, the greatest blessing was being married to the love of her life, Jake, a history professor at the City University. Jake shared her love of cats, and their seven felines were healthy, happy, and full of energy. However, their cats were not your run-of-the-mill housecats. They were extraordinary. The cats each had unique abilities that put them in a realm above that of the normal feline. Surreptitiously, they surfed the internet to provide clues to help their humans solve crimes. Or they stole evidence from criminals, hid it, then brought it out when the proper law enforcement officer would be available.

Scout and Abra were Siamese littermates and former stage performers in a magician's 'Hocus Pocus' show. They possessed an uncanny ability to predict murder. Their death dance was an ominous sight to behold, and not one Katherine ignored.

Iris, a seal-point from an upscale New York City cattery, continued to teach the ropes to Siamese newcomers Dewey and Crowie. The kittens had grown into handsome seal-point adults. They each weighed twelve pounds, a size considered normal for a male, apple-headed Siamese.

Lilac, a hyperactive lilac-point, was airborne most of the time and loved to jump to high places. Abby, the golden-eyed, ruddy ticked Abyssinian, was a major crime solver and had recently solved a million dollar theft. Iris and Abby carried on the tradition of stealing things and hiding them in an old wingback chair, but lately their stolen items were normal household items and not clues to solve an important case.

Stevie Sanders — the son of Erie's crime boss — and his thirteen-year-old daughter Salina had moved into the Foursquare next door without a hitch. Back in Prohibition days, the yellow brick house had been a speakeasy. Salina's gray cat Wolfy Joe was feeling much better, having regained the weight he had lost while eating a poor diet.

Katherine taught her computer class in the pink mansion's basement classroom. She met monthly with Chief London and Margie Cokenberger, the wife of handyman Cokey, to select and approve charitable distributions to people in need in the community. Her no-kill rescue center was a huge success, having found adopters for many homeless cats, dogs, rabbits, a goat and even two llamas.

Yes, things were pretty much working out great in the small town of Erie, Indiana. Until . . . .

Chapter Two

Saturday

Katherine sat behind the wheel of her Subaru Outback while best friend Colleen sat in the passenger seat.

On the back seat, Scout and Abra stood tall in their cat carrier. The felines were not happy traveling in the SUV and voiced their complaints in loud Siamese voices.

Colleen shouted over the din, "Katz, tell me again why we're bringing them?"

"Girls, settle down," Katherine pleaded with the cats. "We'll be there in a minute," she added. Katherine and Jake had rented a two-story farmhouse in the country for two months while the attic of the pink mansion was being remodeled. Jake was thrilled to be getting a new office, not comfortable with the bad vibes in the basement where his current one was. He jokingly called his future office *the man cave in the sky.*

"It goes like this, Carrot Top," Katherine began, addressing her best friend since grade school. "I want Scout's and Abra's opinion on the house."

"Like if it's haunted or not? It makes perfect sense to me." The Siamese were very sensitive to the paranormal.

The feminine GPS voice instructed Katherine to turn right, but Katherine ignored the command and drove past it.

"Shouldn't you have turned back there?" Colleen asked.

The Siamese became agitated. "Waugh," Scout shrieked. "Raw," Abra added. Ever since their move from Manhattan to the small town of Erie, they had zero tolerance for the GPS lady. The two retaliated by rocking the carrier back and forth.

Katherine scolded, "Stop it right now," then to Colleen, "I better turn it off." She reached over and pressed the off button, then pulled previously printed instructions from a cubbyhole in the center floor console. She slowed down to study them.

"You're not supposed to read and drive at the same time," Colleen cautioned.

"Oh, yeah?" Katherine asked, amused. "I haven't seen a car on this road since we left. I guess it's too early for people to be out and about. There it is," she added, nodding to the right. She turned off the state highway and onto a country gravel road. Immediately the road dipped to a steep downgrade and into a ravine. At the bottom was a dense morning fog that hovered over the ground, casting an eerie appearance on the surrounding landscape.

"Wow, this fog just came out of nowhere," Katherine said in a worried tone, she slowed down to ten miles an hour. Without a center line painted on the road, it was difficult to gauge where she was driving.

"Is there a place to pull over?" Colleen advised, leaning forward and clutching the handle on the glove box.

At the top of the next rise, the patchy fog lifted. The narrow country road was flanked on both sides by tall corn plants that were a few weeks away from harvest. Their yellowing leaves gently flapped in the wind. Colleen powered down her window and reached her arm out.

"Slow down. I'd like to pick an ear. Want to have corn for dinner?" she asked naively.

"That's not sweet corn; it's field corn."

"What's the difference?"

"Sweet corn is soft; field corn will break your teeth off."

"And when did you become an expert on corn?"

"Jake and I take the Jeep out on this road. That's how we found the farmhouse we're driving to?"

"Was there a for rent sign in the yard?"

"Jake knows the owner, Bud Baxter."

"Bud? Seriously, someone has a first name, Bud?"

"Mr. Baxter does," Katherine laughed. "He's an elderly man who lives with his wife, who has Parkinson's disease. When we drove up to the farmhouse and didn't see any vehicles, Jake called him. Bud said they'd moved to an assisted living facility in the City."

"Won't it be hard for them to manage both places?"

"They plan to put the farm on the market next spring and wanted to hire someone to keep an eye on it this winter. That's when Jake proposed that we'd rent it."

"Why don't the two of you just stay in the bungalow?" Katherine and Jake owned an early century Craftsman on the next street from the mansion.

"It's not big enough for our cat family."

"Ma-waugh," Scout meowed in agreement.

"Okay," Colleen said slowly. "Here's my next question. Is the farmhouse clean enough to meet your standards?" She chuckled. With seven cats, Katherine worked hard to keep the mansion clean. Being a millionaire didn't change Katherine. She always did her own housework.

"That's why I'm bringing you today. I need some help," Katherine teased.

"Help doing what?" Colleen asked, knowing that cleaning house was not one of her strong suits. "Why don't you hire a cleaning crew?"

"Actually, I did. The house is clean, from the cellar to the top rafters, but today I want you to help me cat proof it."

"How are we going to do that with two cats?"

"Scout and Abra will be on leashes. I need you to mind Abra, while I walk with Scout."

"I've got a bit of experience doing that," Colleen said, then asked, "What's the address of this place?"

"Actually, it's a rural address. Baxter is painted in red letters on the mailbox. The house is set back from the road."

"Which side of the road?"

"It's on the right. Just before we get to it, there's a giant oak tree with branches hanging over the road. Look for a metal gate."

"You're talking like a Hoosier."

Katherine wrinkled her nose, amused. "Jake is a great teacher."

Suddenly, the road changed to a rutted expanse of potholes and ridges. Katherine rumbled over several, then slowed down to a crawl.

Colleen screamed, "Look out!"

A tall, thin man darted across the road, in a dead run, and nearly stumbled into the SUV. He was dressed like a scarecrow. His face was covered with a burlap bag with holes cut out for his eyes and mouth. He wore denim overalls over a red plaid shirt. Straw stuck out of the cuffs. Katherine screamed and hit the brakes.

"Oh, the Saints preserve us. I thought we'd all be killed," Colleen said, holding her hand over her heart.

The man never slowed, but jogged into the cornfield, unfazed by his brush with death.

Katherine pulled over, put the SUV in park, and started to climb out.

Colleen protested. "Katz, no, get back in the car. What if that nut case comes back?"

"I've got to check on the cats." Getting out, she reached inside her summer-weight jacket for her Glock, but instead of pulling it out, she patted the side holster for reassurance, then opened the back door to check on the Siamese. They were very quiet — too quiet. They sat on their haunches with their front paws braced against the cage; Scout had one paw over Abra's shoulder.

"Are you two okay?" Katherine asked worriedly, climbing onto the seat to check on them.

"Raw," Abra cried sweetly.

"Are they all right?" Colleen turned and asked over her shoulder.

"Yes, they look okay. I'm glad I belted the cat carrier to the back seat," Katherine answered, then said to the cats, "I promise, it's just a little ways up the road. We're almost there."

Scout crossed her sapphire-blue eyes and blinked an eye kiss.

Katherine got behind the wheel, shifted to drive and continued at barely five miles an hour. "My heart's pounding a mile a minute."

"Mine too. Thank God we didn't hit him. He seemed oblivious to us," Colleen observed.

"If we did hit him, that would have made an interesting 911 call," Katherine said, then feigned a masculine voice, "Officer, scarecrow down. Send an ambulance."

Colleen piped in, "Or a hay wagon."

Katherine smiled.

"What was he doing out here wearing that outfit?" Colleen asked.

"Scarecrow reenactment? I don't know. I'll ask Jake. Maybe there's a Harvest festival nearby?"

"Seriously?"

Katherine laughed to break the tension. "I'm just making it up as I go. I have no idea, but I know my street sense perked up. I don't think Mr. Scarecrow was up to any good."

"Ma-waugh," Scout agreed.

"Mine did too. Hey, look over there," Colleen pointed.

Katherine gazed out her window at a rusted fence with a gate covered with multiple "do not trespass" signs. There was a gravel area in front of the gate, which was just enough space for a car to park while the owner got out and opened or closed the access.

"Katz, pull into that little area there," Colleen said excitedly. "I want to take a picture."

"Why?"

"Look at those symbols!"

Katherine braked, put the vehicle in reverse, and backed up. She powered down her window and gazed at several rusted metal pentagrams attached to the posts supporting the gate. Several more crude pentagrams, made of rough twigs fastened with twine, were stuck in the ground. She lightly tapped the accelerator, drove in front of the gate, and turned off the engine.

Colleen jumped out and rushed to the farm gate. Katherine stayed in the SUV.

"Katz, aren't you getting out?"

Katherine leaned out the window. "Ah, no. Look at those weeds. They could be full of poison ivy."

"Come on. Stop being a princess. Look at these symbols. This is something you don't see every day."

"Okay. Okay." Katherine unbuckled her seat belt, turned to the back seat, and said to the cats. "This will only take a second."

Scout and Abra pawed the metal gate of their carrier, wanting out.

"These are witch symbols," Colleen announced, fascinated. "The ones stuck in the ground represent the witch from Maryland."

Katherine climbed out of the vehicle, leaned over and examined the sticks. "Looks like somebody's craft project that went bad."

"No, Katz," Colleen said, slightly irritated. "They remind me of that movie, *Blair Witch*."

Katherine started to go back to the SUV. "This creeps me out."

"Wait, back in the 1700s, an elderly woman in Maryland was accused of being a witch. She was shunned by the people in the town and banished to the deep woods."

"Okay, that's interesting. Why don't you come back and tell me in the car."

Colleen continued, "She died there, probably of exposure, and came back to haunt anyone who trespassed in the woods."

Katherine furrowed her brow. "Returning to this century, why on earth would this stuff be out here in the middle of nowhere, stuck to an old gate?"

Colleen took a picture with her cell phone. "The five-pointed star is an ancient symbol of a man with his arms and legs outstretched . . . ."

Katherine and Colleen were startled by the sound of twigs breaking in the nearby grove of trees.

An attractive woman in her late fifties, with long, salt-and-pepper colored hair, stepped out into the clearing. She wore a fashionable pink floral sundress with a pair of matching flip flops. She looked like she stepped off the cover of a fashion magazine, except for the double-barrel shotgun she held in her hands.

"What the hell are you doing on my property?" the woman asked in a hostile manner, pointing the shotgun at them.

Katherine instinctively put her hands up. "I'm sorry," she answered, alarmed. "We meant no harm."

Several black cats, ranging from kittens to adults, followed the woman. A kitten trotted over and wrapped itself around Katherine's leg. It purred loudly. Katherine was too frightened to reach down and pet it.

The woman asked in an angry voice. "Are you the ones defacing my property?" She pointed the gun in the direction of the farm gate.

Katherine shook her head. "I don't understand. What stuff?"

"That witch stuff!"

"No," Katherine answered.

"Then what are you doing here?"

"We almost hit a man who ran right in front of us," Katherine answered, not wanting to mention that he was dressed up like a scarecrow. "I pulled over to check on my cats. They're in a cat carrier on my back seat."

Colleen huddled next to Katherine, and added, "I'm taking a photography class, and thought your gate would make a great, countryside picture."

Katherine looked at Colleen curiously. She'd just caught her friend in a lie. Colleen wasn't taking a photography class. Katherine thought, *That's a brilliant excuse . . . .or not.*

The woman eyed Colleen suspiciously. "You're not from around these parts, are you?"

Colleen slowly shook her head. "No, I moved to Indiana from Queens, New York."

Katherine mentally searched for the right words to defuse the situation, then said hurriedly, "Allow me to introduce myself. My name is Katherine Cokenberger. My husband and I rented the farmhouse up the road from Bud Baxter. My friend and I are on our way there now."

The woman lowered the shotgun and smiled, revealing a beautiful set of white teeth. "Why didn't you say you were Professor Cokenberger's wife?"

"You know my husband?" Katherine asked, surprised. She lowered her arms to normal position.

"Yes, I used to teach at the university. I'm a history professor too. So you're going to be my new neighbors?"

"Just for a few months while we're having work done on our house in Erie."

"Erie? I thought Jake lived on a windmill farm." Katherine shook her head.

The woman continued, "I knew Jake's late wife well. I was her spiritual advisor. I predicted Victoria wouldn't have a long life. I'm also a psychic."

"Interesting," Katherine said, wondering what a spiritual advisor was. She also pondered why Jake never mentioned that his deceased wife consulted a psychic.

"Is Jake writing another book?"

Katherine was taken aback by the question. She wondered why she was now standing in knee-high weeds, having a conversation with a woman holding a gun. She didn't understand the connection between a few months at a farmhouse and Jake writing a book. The woman noticed the change in expression.

"Jake always did that when he was working on something new," the woman explained.

"Katz, I've got to be somewhere in a bit," Colleen urged.

"Sure," Katherine said to Colleen, then turned to the woman. "We'd better take off. I'm anxious to get my cats to the new place. They don't like being in the carrier."

The woman glared at Katherine. "Then don't put them in one. My cats are free. I never confine them."

The clowder of black cats began to meow. Scout and Abra did too. The Siamese loud complaints from the SUV were muffled but still audible.

Katherine looked back in the direction of her vehicle, then reached down and petted the kitten that wouldn't stop nudging her leg. Two more cats —

tortoiseshells — slinked out from behind a tree. Katherine petted them too.

"The black kitten's name is Sabrina. Over there is her mama, Isadora. She's part Siamese."

A long, slender black version of Scout and Abra slinked over and rubbed against the woman's leg. The cat had a wedge-shaped face, pointed ears and almond-shaped eyes.

"She's very sleek. I love her shiny fur," Katherine admired. "Aren't they called Oriental shorthairs?"

"I don't care what they call them. Isadora is part Siamese. Her mama was a seal-point," the woman corrected. "The large black one is Amara. I haven't named the Tortie girls yet. They just came to me."

Colleen's eyes widened. "Came to you?" she asked.

"I never turn away a homeless cat."

"How many cats do you have?" Katherine asked out of curiosity, in a friendly voice.

"Why do you want to know?" the woman asked guardedly.

"Curious like a cat," Katherine smiled. "I funded the Erie Animal Rescue Center, and —"

The woman became disturbed. "Wait a minute? I get it. You're that rich New Yorker who lives in the pink house."

Katherine sensed renewed hostility from the woman. She worried that the woman would point the gun at them again.

"You work at the new animal center, which totally explains why you're here. To check me out!" she spat. "You want to know if I'm a cat hoarder?"

"What? Why no," Katherine answered cautiously, trying not to appear too angry at being accused of saying something she didn't say.

"You go back and tell that no-good, liar Dr. Goodwin to mind his freaking business. I've just enough cats I can afford to take care of in the manner they richly deserve."

"Seriously, I'm not here in an official capacity. I funded the Center; I'm not an employee there." Katherine smacked a hungry mosquito off her arm. She'd already sustained numerous bites on her legs and regretted that she hadn't sprayed herself with repellent. But, then again, her plan was to go directly to the farmhouse and not have a chit-chat with a woman brandishing a shotgun. She started to inch toward the SUV. "It was nice meeting you," she began. "Oh, how rude of me, I've forgotten your name."

"That's because I didn't give it," the woman answered insolently. Then, in an instant change of mood, said amiably, "I'm sorry. I don't mean to be rude. My name is Elizabeth, but I go by Lizzie. Give my love to Jake. He's a prince of all men. If you'll excuse me, I've got to feed my cats." The woman started to turn, but stopped. "The farmhouse is just around the bend. Have a pleasant day." She took off down the lane with the cats following her, darting in and out around her legs. She murmured to them in a low voice, then started humming a tune that sounded like the theme song from the movie *Rosemary's Baby.*

Katherine grabbed Colleen by the arm, and quickly directed her back to the SUV. Colleen rushed to the passenger side and jumped in.

Katherine climbed in and started the engine. Backing out, she said, "First the scarecrow, then the witch packing a gun, this is too much for one trip."

"Raw," Abra agreed.

"Hurry up, Katz. Floor it. Let's get out of here. There's something not right with that woman. Why would those witch symbols be on her gate?"

"Better question: Why was she humming the theme song to *Rosemary's Baby?*"

"What?"

"The movie about the witches."

"You're right. Shut the door! What's with all the black cats?"

"Maybe she's a witch," Katherine said in a mysterious voice. "Her black kitten was named after the teenage witch Sabrina."

"T'is a mystery," Colleen said, shaking her head. "At first she said she was a history professor, then she said she was a spiritual advisor."

"I need to find out what she's got against Dr. Goodwin."

"Who?"

"The Director of the Rescue Center."

"She seemed awful chummy about Jake," Colleen observed.

"I noticed that. Not that I'm jealous, but she's gorgeous."

"Katz, you've got her beat in the looks department."

"Aww, thank you. That was sweet." She laughed nervously, then pointed, "There's the lane to the farmhouse."

"Is the gate supposed to be open?" Colleen asked, looking at the metal farmer's gate that had been moved to the side.

"Oh, I forgot to tell you. Jake drove out here earlier. The Baxters left some of their antique furniture, so Jake's moving it into a room."

"Why?"

"So the cats don't scratch it. We'll keep the room shut up so the cats can't get in there."

"How are you going to do that with Scout the Houdini cat?"

"Waugh," Scout cried, adding her two cents.

"Jake's supposed to install an interlocking deadbolt on the door, or else Scout will be in that storage room in a New York minute."

Katherine turned into the lane, then stopped. She fished her cell phone from the back pocket of her khaki pants.

Colleen asked impatiently, "Why are we stopping?"

"I'm texting Chief London."

"Why Chief London?"

"Someone is vandalizing that woman's place. She was friendly to us because she knows Jake, but what if she doesn't know the person? She shouldn't be pointing a gun at anyone."

"Katz, I know enough about the law. She had every legal right to point the gun at us because we were trespassing."

"Na-waugh," Scout disagreed.

Colleen continued, "Chief London and the Erie police don't have jurisdiction out here. This is a county matter. You need to contact Sheriff what's his name."

"Sheriff Johnson."

"Raw," Abra complained, pawing the front of the carrier.

"The troops are getting restless. I'll call him after I get the cats settled in the house."

Chapter Three

The Director of the Erie Animal Rescue Center
drove his Mercedes-Benz sedan into his reserved parking
spot, parked, and lifted a red rose off the console. Dr.
Goodwin walked briskly to the building, inserted his key,
and made his way to the back of the hall where the laundry
room was located. The object of his affection was a
middle-aged woman leaning over a sink scrubbing litter
boxes. He ran over and threw his arms around her.

"Get off of me, you idiot," she said, then laughed.
"You nearly scared me to death. I thought I was the only
one in the building."

"I just got here, and wanted to give you a squeeze
before the other weekend volunteers show up."

"It amazes me how you can come into the building
and not wake up the dogs. When I first arrived, they went
nuts barking."

"I'm as quiet as a mouse," he winked.

"Is that for me?" she said, reaching for the rose.

"I'm afraid you'll have to work for it," he said, hiding the rose behind his back.

"Give it to me, you fool." She leaned forward, yanked the rose out of his hand and smelled it.

"Did anyone ever tell you how sexy you are?" he asked, drawing the woman near.

"Yes, all my lovers, especially when I'm washing litter boxes. Go figure."

He kissed her long and hard. "I love it when you talk that way."

"What way is that?"

"When you talk about your lovers, it really turns me on."

"We'll work on that later," she said in a sultry voice, then added in a more serious tone. "When are you going to help me get my stuff from my husband?"

"Your ex," the director corrected her.

"He would have *never* left me for that witch if she hadn't cast a spell on him."

"Melinda," he began gently. "Nicholas has been missing for quite some time. I'm thinking he's probably dead."

"He can't be declared legally dead until his body is found," she said indignantly. "I can't wait any longer. I want what's entitled to me."

"My sexy girl, must I remind you that you're divorced. Do you still have a thing for him?" he asked, changing gears.

"No sugar," she said coyly. "My thing is with you. I just want what belongs to me."

"I can buy anything you want. Do I look poor?"

"I'm not asking you to murder her —"

"Well, that's good because murder isn't my cup of tea."

"If you want any more sugar in your tea, you'll do what I ask," she answered seductively. Returning to the sink, she rinsed the bin and set it on the floor. Looking up, she said, "I think I've come up with a way to lure that woman out of her house —"

"You mean Lizzie?" he interrupted, running his eyes up and down the woman.

"Once you get her out of the house, I can go in, open the safe, and get back my stuff."

"How do you know that Lizzie didn't change the combination? How do you know if your stuff is still there?"

"Before Nicholas went missing, he said he'd bring it to me."

"Bring what?"

"My late mom's wedding ring."

"Why haven't you told me this before? Why is this so important that you want me to risk my neck to help you?"

"Tony, the ring was the only thing of value that my mom gave me. I wore it on my pinky for good luck. I lost it in the house before I moved out. Nicholas found it a few days before he disappeared. He called and said he wanted to meet me somewhere so he could give it to me."

"After all these years, why don't you just ask Lizzie for it?"

"I'd rather break that woman's neck then ask her for anything," she said venomously.

"No need to get upset, precious," he said, stroking the back of her long red hair.

Melinda fought back tears, "I'll only be in the house for a minute. You don't have to kidnap Lizzie or do anything that drastic. It's a win-win, in-and-out situation."

"Do you have a plan in mind? Because I certainly don't. I've got other fish to fry with this woman."

"You mean the cat hoarding? Everyone in town is talking about it."

"I'm calling the sheriff about it this morning."

"That's good. Don't forget to mention she uses her cats as familiars to bewitch her enemies."

"Precious, you know I don't believe that supernatural stuff. I think she's a witch, but I don't mean it literally."

Melinda frowned, then brightened as she thought through her plan. "Tomorrow is the flea market in Millbridge."

"So?"

"Lizzie has a booth there. That gives me a couple of hours to get inside her house and look around."

"What's my role in this?"

"I need you to drive to Millbridge and make sure she's there, then call me."

"I can't do that."

"Why not?"

"My wife and I have plans tomorrow. I can't get away. Besides, wouldn't it be more practical for you to watch Lizzie leave, then go in her house?"

Melinda looked up at the ceiling. "How am I goin' to do that? She'll see my car," she said in irritated disbelief.

"I don't mean park at the gate. There's a farmer's service lane across the road. If you drive in far enough, the cornfield will hide you. Do you remember how to get to the house?"

"No, I'm suffering from amnesia," she answered sarcastically. "Of course, I remember. I used to live there, sweetness. I know a shortcut."

"You know this is crazy, insane," he said. "I love ya, but if you get caught, I won't vouch for you."

"Vouch for me?" she asked, miffed. "Trust me. I won't implicate you in any way."

"I'm not going to lose my job and my veterinarian license for a ring."

"Fine," Melinda said sharply. "I can do this myself. Sorry I bothered you with it."

"Don't be that way," he said, trying to hug her.

She moved aside. "Don't touch me," she pouted.

"I'm sorry, Melinda. I don't want to quarrel. I'll see you Monday," he said, starting to leave.

"I'll text you when I get the ring?"

"Not a good idea. I've talked to you about that. More marriages end in divorce from inappropriate text messages than from anything else. Don't you pay attention to the news?"

"Okay, then I'll send you an emoticon of a ring," she said, then her eyes grew big, and she stepped back. "Shhh, the dogs just started barking. Someone must have come in. Better get out of here before anyone sees us."

"Later," he said, leaving the room. He closed the door behind him and walked to his office next door. Sitting down at his desk, he tugged his cell from his jacket's pocket and punched in the sheriff's direct number.

Sheriff Johnson answered in a clipped voice, "Dr. Goodwin. How may I help you?"

"How'd you know it was me?"

"I saw your name pop up on my screen. What's up?"

The director paused for a split second, surprised at the sheriff's to-the-point greeting. "We've got a potential cat hoarding situation —"

"I'll stop you right there. Potential means maybe. Is or isn't. Is there a cat hoarding situation in Erie County

or not?" the sheriff asked, in a 'just-give-me-the-facts'
manner.

"I've had several people call and complain about a
woman in the country who has as many as a hundred cats."

"A hundred cats?" the sheriff asked skeptically.
"How did folks come up with that number?"

"I'm not sure how they arrived at that figure, but
I've driven out to the property several times. The owner is
antagonistic and won't let me past the front gate. I need to
investigate to see whether these allegations are true or not."

"Sounds like you're trying to do my job," the sheriff
answered testily. "Who are we talking about?"

"Elizabeth Howe. People call her Lizzie."

"Yes, I know," the sheriff said, then paused. "I'm
very familiar with Ms. Howe. I know that you're not from
Erie, so I'll fill you in. Several years ago I investigated the
disappearance of her husband. I can assure you, that at that
time, Ms. Howe didn't have a hundred cats. I was in her
house many times. I saw a few, but they looked mighty
fine to me."

"Sheriff, a person's mental state can change overnight. Cat hoarding is a psychological problem."

The sheriff answered irritably, "You're making a very strong accusation based on a few irate phone calls."

"Sheriff, I'm not trying to do your job. I meant no disrespect. I just want to have the legal authority to go in, have a look-see and gather information."

"What kind of information?" the sheriff asked.

"On the number of cats she has and their welfare. If this woman is hoarding that many cats, the Rescue Center needs to be prepared for the intake."

"I'm more than happy to execute a search warrant, but you need to meet with the prosecutor and trust me, he'll want more evidence to present to the judge than a couple of irate phone calls."

"I have a petition signed by seventy people —"

"I didn't realize that many people lived out that way," the sheriff interrupted.

"I must reiterate. Lizzie Howe is a hoarder," he said, then paused, waiting for the sheriff to answer, but when he didn't, he continued, "It's imperative that I get out there and see what's going on."

"Is Katherine Cokenberger aware of this situation?"

"I haven't brought her up-to-speed yet."

"I suggest you do."

"I have the authority to act alone," Dr. Goodwin replied, slightly offended.

"She's got a lot of influence in this neck of the woods."

"Yes, yes, I'm aware of that."

"In the meantime, it's my day off and my wife and I are hittin' the golf course."

"Thank you so much for your time. I'll get back to you."

The sheriff hung up without answering.

Chapter Four

Katherine slid her cell back in her pocket, tapped the gas pedal and drove down the rented farmhouse's gravel drive. A cloud of dust trailed after her. The curvy lane was flanked on both sides by the tall corn.

Colleen leaned forward in her seat. "I don't see the house. All I see is corn."

The Siamese became very active. "Raw," Abra belted. It sounded like 'hurry up, let's just get there already.'

Katherine drove to a clearing and parked next to a one-car garage. Jake's Jeep Wrangler was parked inside with the garage door open.

The farmhouse loomed like a giant limestone fortress. The two-story house was built on an elevated stone foundation, which made it even higher. A wooden front porch sported a porch swing, which made the house idyllic in Katherine's mind. She loved porch swings.

Jake sat on the top step. When he saw Katherine and Colleen approaching, he waved and hurried off the front porch to greet them.

"Hey, Sweet Pea," he said, opening Katherine's door and helping her out of the vehicle. "How are you, Colleen? How's my cousin Daryl doing?"

Colleen glanced at her feet, then looked up, and said tartly, "I wouldn't have a clue. I haven't seen him for a bit."

Jake's eyes widened in surprise. He started to say something, but Katherine nudged his arm. "Can you take Scout and Abra inside?"

"Of course," he said, kissing her cheek. "I've got their room all ready for them."

"Raw," Abra, now happy their journey had ended, cried sweetly, rubbing her brown mask against the gate of the cat carrier. Scout did the same.

"How are my baby girls?" Jake said in a soft voice. He carefully removed the carrier and walked to the house.

After he was out of earshot, Katherine asked Colleen, "What's going on? What do you mean you haven't seen Daryl in a while?"

Colleen waited until Jake walked into the house, then answered sadly. "I think Daryl is getting ready to dump me."

"What?" Katherine almost shrieked in disbelief.

"He just doesn't seem like the man I fell in love with. He's distant. We go out to dinner and he doesn't talk to me. Oh, he's polite and everything, like all the Cokenberger men, but when I ask him a question and try to pull him into a conversation, he hardly answers back with yes or no. He's like that all the time. It's like he doesn't want to talk to me."

"Have you asked him about it?"

"It doesn't do any good. If we go out to dinner with another couple, Daryl never shuts up, but as soon as we're alone he becomes very quiet . . . I can't explain it."

"I'm sorry to hear this. Let me know if I can be of any help."

"If that means, talking to Jake who'll talk to Daryl, no thanks."

"Oh, I'd never," Katherine began, then muttered under her breath, "Unless, Colleen, you wanted me to."

"Katz, where's the bat room?" Colleen asked abruptly, changing the subject.

Katherine laughed at her friend's pronunciation. "Bat room is the first door on the left."

Colleen ran into the farmhouse, slamming the screen door behind her. "Oops, I didn't mean to do that," she called through the door.

Jake came out of the house and met Katherine on the top step. "I was getting worried about you. What took you so long?"

"Oh, the usual stuff. Nothing eventful," Katherine said with a mischievous glint in her eye.

Jake motioned to the swing. "My lady," he said, bowing.

Katherine walked over and sat down. She patted the space next to her, "Milord." When Jake sat down, the chain chinked.

"Whoa. This swing better not fall."

"It won't. I double-checked it. Get back to why you were late."

Colleen came out and poured herself into a wicker side chair. "That's quite a place in there," she admired, then asked. "Did I interrupt something?"

Katherine shook her head. "I was about to tell Jake our gut-wrenching story."

"Oh, I can do that," Colleen said. "For starters, Katz came an inch from hitting a man dressed in a scarecrow outfit."

"What?" Jake asked. "You two been hitting the margarita bar?"

"I'm not drunk," Colleen continued. "He ran across the road and Katz jammed on the brakes. A bit later, I saw this farm gate with witch symbols on it. I asked Katz to stop so I could take a picture."

Jake asked, "Where was this?"

"The property on the left, just before you get to the farmhouse," Katherine joined in. "Jake, a woman pointed a shotgun at us and accused us of vandalizing her property. She said she knows you."

"What?" Jake asked incredulously. "Professor Howe pointed a gun at you?"

"Who is this woman?"

"Elizabeth Howe. The locals call her Lizzie. Last year, she took early retirement from the university. She's somewhat of an eccentric, but rumor has it that a lot of academics, including me, have taken a walk on the odd side one time or another."

"That's not true," Katherine defended. "You're not odd."

Jake grinned. "How many other professors do you know who dress up like John Dillinger to teach their class on Prohibition?"

Colleen interjected, smiling. "Or marry a woman with cats that surf the internet."

"Colleen," Katherine scolded, looking shocked.

"Well, it's true. I'm not daft."

"This is —

"Top secret," Colleen finished. "I wouldn't tell anyone. Who'd believe me?"

Jake winked. "Colleen, I beg to differ. I married Katz for her beat-up Toyota."

"Yeah, right," Katherine mused. "We hadn't even started dating when the tornado flattened my car. Tell us more about Professor Howe."

"Even in the dead of winter, with a foot of snow on the ground, she'd walk around campus wearing her signature flip flops."

"She wore flip flops today," Colleen noted.

Jake continued, "It was embarrassing to the University's powers-that-be because she'd attend high-level academic meetings dressed in a torn calico farm dress."

"I wouldn't even know what a calico farm dress looks like," Katherine said.

"Google it, Sweet Pea."

"Sounds like the *powers-that-be* were snobs," she added.

"It wasn't so much the ratty clothes but the fact she'd bring incense, light it, and wave it around the room before she sat down. After the meeting, she'd ask if anyone wanted their fortunes told."

Katherine brought her hand up to stifle a laugh. "Maybe we should hire her for our next Halloween party."

Colleen said, "I'm convinced the woman is daft."

"She's eccentric, but not daft. She's very intelligent and highly respected in her field."

"What field is that?" Katherine asked. "Ballistics? Did she write a textbook on how to shoot your neighbors with a double-barreled shotgun?"

"Her expertise is early American history. She taught a very popular "history of witchcraft" class, and even held a mock Salem witchcraft trial."

Colleen and Katherine exchanged curious glances.

"Is she married?" Katherine asked.

"She met her third husband —"

"Third husband!" Colleen interrupted. "I can't even snag one," she added with resignation.

"Go on, Jake," Katherine prodded.

"Her third husband is, I mean, was an electrical engineer. He went missing several years ago. There was a thorough sheriff investigation but he just vanished off the face of the earth. Someone started a rumor that Elizabeth murdered him, and buried him somewhere on her property."

"Who would say such a thing?" Katherine asked with disapproval.

"I don't know, but it caught on like wildfire."

Colleen asked, "Do people ever call her a witch? She does have black cats."

"Poor Elizabeth has been called a murderer and a witch. As for the black cats, she has always been a cat person."

"Historically, black cats are associated with witchcraft and evil," Colleen instructed.

Katherine countered, "Just because Lizzie has black cats doesn't mean she's a witch."

"If she's not a witch, why would anyone put witch symbols on her gate?" Colleen inquired.

Katherine shrugged her shoulders. "Maybe Lizzie put them there herself. I noticed the pentagrams were pretty rusty and looked like they'd been there for a while."

"That doesn't make any sense," Colleen retorted. "She was truly angry and accused us of putting them there."

"I'd say whoever fastened the signs to the gate has a serious grudge," Jake offered.

"Who could that be? Why would anyone want to deface someone's property with that stuff?" Katherine asked.

"When I drove by, I didn't look at Professor Howe's gate. I'll check it out when I drive home. However, I'm concerned that this sort of vandalism can accelerate into something violent, especially since Elizabeth feels compelled to protect her property."

Katherine touched Jake on the arm. "Go back to the part about her third husband going missing."

"When her husband disappeared, she retired, and moved out to the country."

"Why here?" Colleen asked.

"This property belonged to her late husband, assuming he's dead."

"What's his name?" Katherine and Colleen asked at the same time.

"Nicholas Howe. When they first got married, Nicholas and Elizabeth would drive out here to their cabin for weekend retreats. The house is very primitive looking on the outside —"

"You've been there?" Katherine asked quizzically.

"Several times."

Colleen gave an "Uh-huh, I told you so" glance to Katherine.

Jake saw the look. "Professor Howe hosted several faculty picnics there. On the inside, the cabin is very modern."

"How can a cabin be modern?" Katherine asked, remembering the cabin she'd rented for a long weekend where everything appeared to be out of a rustic furniture catalog.

"The walls were smooth and painted gray. The kitchen had stainless steel appliances with granite countertops. There was a big screen TV over the fireplace mantel. Nicholas used solar panels, and some pretty sophisticated gadgets, to provide electricity and to heat the place in winter. Elizabeth preferred to stay in their apartment close to campus, and not live out here full-time. She'd join Nicholas on the weekends."

"I wonder what changed her mind?" Katherine asked.

"Peaceful country livin'," Jake said in an exaggerated Hoosier twang.

Katherine wrinkled her nose in amusement.

"Reckon I best be leavin'," he continued the fake accent. He got up from the porch swing. "Well, ladies, I must head back to Erie. Nice seeing you, Colleen."

Colleen smiled. "You too, Jake."

Jake leaned over and kissed Katherine on the forehead. "I'll see you when I see you."

"We probably won't stay long. I'll text you when we're heading back."

Jake descended the steps and walked down a dirt path to the one-car garage. He backed his Jeep out, honked, then drove down the lane.

"Okay, let's get the show on the road," Katherine said, getting up and making her way to the door. Colleen got up, stretched and followed.

Katherine walked to the room where the Siamese were and opened the door. The cats sat on a wide windowsill and swiveled their brown-pointed ears in the direction of the door. "Raw," Abra cried with apprehension. She made a beeline to escape.

"Abra, stop! Not yet. Quick, Colleen, shut the door before the two of them get out and go running amok." Katherine reached into her bag and removed two leashes. She leaned down and attached the leash to Abra's rhinestone-studded collar, picked the Siamese up, and gently handed her to Colleen.

Colleen took the cat in her arms and started to talk to her in a gentle voice, "You're a sweet little lass."

Katherine walked over and fastened the leash to Scout's collar. She was surprised that Scout didn't move an inch. The Siamese was gazing intently at something outside the window and wasn't in the least bit interested in taking a walk.

"At-at-at-at-at!" Scout clucked.

"Scout, what are you looking at?" Katherine asked, squinting through the window. She leaned forward and scanned the cornfield that bordered the west side of the house. She thought she saw someone standing at the edge of the field, past a dilapidated shed, but when she did a double take, whoever it was had vanished into the corn rows.

"What the hell?" she asked, frightened.

Scout began swaying back-and-forth on the wide windowsill, clearly agitated. Abra leaped out of Colleen's arms and joined Scout on the window sill.

Colleen moved over and looked out. "What's the matter?"

"I thought I saw someone standing in the field."

"Shut the door? The scarecrow?"

"No, not a man, but a woman."

"All I see are corn plants."

"Look. Right there," Katherine pointed. "Past that red-painted shed."

"I see it, but it's not a person, it's a very large cat."

The black cat turned and disappeared into the cornfield. Several other black cats sprung out from behind the shed and followed.

"I see them now."

"At-at-at-at-at!" Scout repeated.

"Is that Lizzie's cats?" Colleen asked.

"I don't know."

"The big one looked like Amara."

"Your memory amazes me. I was too worried about being shot to remember all the cat's names. I'll ask Jake to call the Baxters to see if they left their cats behind. I pray they didn't."

"What do you mean?"

"They've been away for a while. If those cats belong to them, who's been feeding them?"

"But, Katz, the cats were black. What are the odds of the Baxters having black cats as well? Maybe it was Lizzie you saw walk into the cornfield."

Katherine shook her head. "I couldn't tell."

"Would she have time to walk over here? I know she lives next door, but that's quite a hike, and why would she be trespassing on this property?"

"I have absolutely no idea."

Colleen's brows arched with concern. "Maybe we should go."

Suddenly spooked, Katherine asked, "Did you lock the front door?"

"I can't remember if I did or not," Colleen said warily.

Katherine, always concerned about security, bolted out of the room to the front door. She engaged the antique latch, then moved to the front west parlor to take a look again. This time a gentle breeze made the corn plants sway.

Colleen asked, uneasy. "Are you sure you saw someone?"

"I know I'm not seeing things. Scout saw it too."

"So what's the plan now? The cats are freaked out. Don't you think we should stop the cat-proofing mission and just go home?"

A muffled voice sounded from a room deeper in the house. Katherine reached in her jacket and pulled out her Glock.

Colleen said hurriedly, "You were packin' the entire time and didn't let that crazy Lizzie woman know it?"

Katherine put her finger to her lips to quiet Colleen and motioned for her to stay behind.

Cautiously moving down the narrow hallway, gripping her pistol in both hands, Katherine noticed the storage room door standing wide open. She glanced at the deadbolt and realized Jake had installed it too low on the door. She instantly suspected Scout had stood on her back legs, turned the twist knob with her paws, and then pried the door open. Maybe it was a two-cat operation with Abra helping.

Before entering the room, Katherine called the cats. "Scout . . . Abra."

"Waugh," Scout cried.

Walking through the door, Katherine noticed the Siamese were perched on an office desk beside a vintage reel-to-reel tape recorder with a microphone plugged into it. Abra had stepped on one of the machine's buttons and was vocalizing. "Raw! Raw! Raw!" she cried in rapid machine-gun intonation.

"Waugh," Scout replied, annoyed, pawing the stop button.

Katherine laughed, put her gun back in its side holster and called to Colleen, "It's okay. The cats found an old tape recorder."

Colleen cautiously joined Katherine in the room. "What did you say?"

Katherine walked over to the machine, pressed reverse, then the play button. The recorded voice of Abra rang loud and clear.

Abra looked up proudly and crossed her deep blue eyes.

Katherine praised, "Abra, you're such a smart girl."

Scout, not liking Abra getting all the attention, boxed Abra's ears, and then jumped down.

"This place is giving me the nervous nellies," Colleen said, relieved. "How did Abra know to do that?"

"Probably something she learned from the magician's show. Maybe it was part of one of the acts."

Abra sat on her haunches and slowly blinked an eye kiss.

Katherine patted her on the head and reached over to pet Scout as well, but Scout was gone.

"Colleen, where's Scout?"

"She flew out the door. She won't be hard to find dragging that leash around."

"You probably just jinxed it?"

Something mechanical came to a screeching halt at the far end of the house.

"Where's that sound coming from?" Colleen asked.

"I think Scout's in the kitchen."

Katherine and Colleen rushed into the room to find Scout sitting inside a wood-sided dumbwaiter; her leash dangled over the edge. The insert door to the dumbwaiter lay on the floor.

"Ma-waugh," Scout cried, assuming her meerkat pose. She rubbed the side of her jaw on the opening.

Katherine scanned the room. The farmhouse kitchen had not been updated in decades. There were no traditional cabinets, just wood shelves built on the walls, and several stand-alone hutches, with glass fronts, that stored glasses, dishes, pots and pans. An Indiana-made Hoosier cabinet with a zinc top counter stood in the corner. The cabinet had been painted white and had decals of fruit pasted on it. A louvered door was half open over the counter top.

Near the tall double hung window was an oak farmer's table with four caned chairs. The aged linoleum floor was in good, clean condition, but was uneven and gently sloped to the back door. That's when Katherine saw that it was ajar, and she lunged to close it.

She muttered, "I can't believe Jake left the door open. He knew I was bringing Scout and Abra. What if they'd gotten out?"

Colleen defended Jake. "He probably got distracted by something. Maybe he wanted to air the room out. It's a bit stuffy."

Katherine said, still annoyed, "He could have opened the window," then when she noticed the window didn't have a screen, she said, "or naught."

Abra leaped onto the Hoosier's zinc top and began sniffing the corner of the bottom shelf. She wrinkled her face in disgust, then turned her attention to Scout.

Colleen, standing closest to the dumbwaiter, grabbed Scout around the stomach and held her tight. "You vixen," she said affectionately. "How did you pry that door off?"

Scout sneezed.

Katherine walked over and took Scout from Colleen's arms. She brushed a cobweb off of the Siamese's nose. "Scout, how did you even know *that* was in here?"

Colleen scrutinized the dumbwaiter. "Do you think this UP arrow on the side works?" she asked, leaning over and pushing the button.

"Don't!" Katherine warned, but it was too late. The dumbwaiter slowly ascended to the top floor and came to a creaking halt. Not wanting the cats to venture into the opening, Katherine snatched the insert door off the floor.

With one hand, she pressed it back in place, and moved the metal turn-buttons to keep the door in place.

"I'd expect a dumbwaiter in a mansion, but an old farmhouse?" Colleen asked.

"Maybe back in the day, someone was bedridden and couldn't use the stairs to come down and eat."

"T'would be easier on the cook to send up a meal rather than carry a tray upstairs, granted someone was up there to receive it."

"Maybe a nurse? Don't know. Just one of those mysteries associated with an old house. Reach over and press that button again."

"Do I have to? That noise was worse than fingernails scraping across a blackboard."

"Well, we can't just leave it up there," Katherine complained.

Colleen smirked, then pressed the DOWN arrow button.

The dumbwaiter slowly descended, squeaking all the way until it rested on the planked base.

Scout struggled to be free.

"Oh, no you don't."

"I guess we need to add this to our cat-proofing list. Number one: Jake needs to install a lock on the dumbwaiter."

Katherine added, "Number two: Jake needs to mount the deadbolt to the storage room a little bit higher, so Scout can't get her paws on it."

Colleen chuckled. "Round One of Scout versus the locksmith." She picked up Abra from the Hoosier. "Can we go now? I'm starving. I vote we take these two back to Erie and then head to the diner."

"Sounds like a plan. It's Saturday, so their special is homemade chicken and noodles."

"Okay, you're killing me."

"But first, I want to go outside and investigate before we go."

"This is the part where you're scaring me — again."

"I'm armed, so don't worry."

"What are you going to do?"

"Check out the place in the field where I saw the person stand. If I find footprints, then I'll know I'm not seeing things."

"Shouldn't you text Jake and tell him what's going on?"

"Why? Nothing's going on. I'm just curious. Listen before I go, help me put these two in the carrier."

"Sure."

"And once we've got them in there, go around and turn out the lights."

"Yes, commander."

"Sorry. I don't mean to be bossy. Please?" Holding Scout, Katherine moved to the front room. She gingerly put the Siamese in the carrier, took Abra from Colleen's arms, and placed Abra next to Scout. The Siamese sat down grasshopper-style and began grooming each other. "I'll be back in a minute," she said, leaving.

Katherine jogged down the porch steps and walked to the edge of the cornfield. She immediately noticed how close together the corn plants were. She wondered if a person could even walk between the rows. She leaned down and scrutinized the area. Finding only cat tracks, she returned to the house.

"Well?" Colleen asked, picking up her bag that was lying on the entry door chair.

"Nada, it must have been my imagination. Are we ready?"

"Yes."

"Raw," Abra cried in a half yawn.

Together, Katherine and Colleen lifted the carrier, moved it to the Subaru, and placed it on the back seat. Katherine ran back to the house and made sure the ancient lockset was locked. She inserted the filigreed-brass key and turned it to the right. Taking out the key, she tested the door handle several times just to be sure, then ran back to the SUV.

Climbing into the driver's seat, she showed the key to Colleen. "It's really old. I'm afraid it will break in the lock someday soon."

Colleen took the key and tried to bend it. "It's stronger than it looks. I don't think I've ever seen a key like this. It looks like something from a Harry Potter movie."

"I know. It's three million years old. Bud Baxter won't allow Jake and me to change the lock or put on another one."

"Why? He let Jake install one on the storage room door."

"He said that the front door is made of a rare mahogany and he didn't want more holes drilled into it."

Colleen became very quiet.

Katherine looked at her curiously. "I know what you're thinking."

Colleen answered tartly, "That's for me to know and you to *not* find out."

"We'll be safe out here."

"I hope you didn't just jinx it," Colleen said under her breath.

"I heard that!" Katherine said.

"Waugh," Scout added in a tone tinged with worry.

Chapter Five

Sunday

The following morning, in the kitchen of the pink mansion, Jake stood behind the stove and flipped two blueberry pancakes onto a plate. Katherine sat at the glass-topped table, drinking hazelnut coffee. The seven cats were on the floor, arranged in a circle, eating their breakfast off small Havilland china plates.

"Yum! Yum!" Iris cried, smacking her lips.

"Mao, mao, mao," Dewey belted.

Jake asked curiously, "Any particular reason why you're interested in an angel Lladro figurine?"

"Lladro? My great-aunt collected them but I don't. Why do you ask?"

"The cats must have surfed up that page. When I walked in your office this morning, it was on your screen."

"When I first moved into the mansion, one of the cats broke a figurine. I packed up the rest of the collection and stored them in the attic."

"Maybe the cats think you're an angel. I do," Jake grinned, setting the plate of pancakes in front of Katherine. "*Bon appetit*," he said in a fake French accent.

"Aren't you going to have any?"

"I've already had breakfast while you and the kids slept in." Jake sat down, picked up the front page of the Sunday newspaper. Scanning it, and not finding anything of interest, he asked, "What time is Scout's and Abra's appointment at the vet on Tuesday?"

"Shhh," Katherine said. "They know what you're saying."

"Na-waugh," Scout protested, no longer interested in her food. She tried to bury it on the ceramic tile floor.

"See what I mean," Katherine said to Jake, then to Scout. "It's not today, sweetie."

An 'I don't believe you' look flashed across Scout's face.

Jake eyes crinkled affectionately on both sides.

"The appointment is at four-thirty. When's your last class?"

"I'll be home by then."

"After you-know-who gets their S-H-O-Ts," Katherine spelled, "I don't plan on driving back to the mansion. I plan to drive straight to the farmhouse."

"Okay, while you're at the V-E-T, I'll move the other cats to the farmhouse. We'll start dinner for you."

"I like that idea," Katherine smiled.

"Na-waugh," Scout repeated. She trotted over and rubbed Katherine's leg.

Katherine scratched Scout's chin. "Eat your breakfast, sweetie. If you don't, Dewey will."

Iris looked up from her bowl and cried a low throaty growl, then the front doorbell clanged.

"Who could that be?" Katherine asked, startled.

"Probably Dad. He's bringing his pickup so we can move a few pieces of furniture to the farmhouse."

"Okay, that's great. Iris and Abby will appreciate their wingback chair being moved. I don't think they'd be happy without a place to hide their loot."

Jake laughed. "I better get the door before Dad rings the bell again."

The cats hated the doorbell worse than the GPS lady.

Jake left the room, but came back in a minute. "Katz, its Dr. Goodwin."

Katherine patted her napkin to her chin where a dollop of butter had fallen. "I wonder what he wants?" she asked, puzzled.

Jake shrugged. "I seated him in the living room. He sat down in the most fragile chair in the room," he smirked.

"Why do big men always do that?" Katherine joked, hoping Dr. Goodwin wouldn't collapse the chair and fall to the floor.

"While you're gone, I'll protect your pancakes from feline fangs and paws."

Abby chirped and then ran her pink tongue over her lips.

"I saw that," Katherine giggled. She got up and made her way to the living room. She tried to shut the door to the kitchen, so the cats wouldn't follow her, but Iris darted past her.

"Miss Siam, come back here," she said, closing the door.

"Yowl," the Siamese sassed, galloping to the front. The defiant cat darted into the living room, and headed straight to the veterinarian.

Dr. Goodwin reached down to pet the escapee. "She's a beautiful Siamese," he admired.

Iris did figure eights in front of the director, purring loudly. Then she moved to the back of the Eastlake side chair he was sitting on. She stood on her hind legs and reached through the gap between the chair's seat and back. She moved her paw with a quickness worthy of a professional pickpocket and removed something from the side pocket of Dr. Goodwin's jacket. Clutching the stolen item in her teeth, she ran underneath the famous wingback chair. Katherine noticed it immediately but didn't try to retrieve the object. Something about Iris's body language warned her not to. Iris caught her glance, and did a slow blink.

Sitting down on the velvet loveseat, Katherine answered, "Iris is special."

"Is Iris the cat who was kidnapped? The one Barbie Sanders took care of?"

"Yes, I'm surprised you know about that."

"Talk is cheap and plentiful in a small town," he laughed.

"What can I help you with today?" Katherine asked, trying to speed up the conversation and get to the point. She had a lot of work to do before the move to the farmhouse. She wondered why the director of one of her charities had dropped by. She knew it wasn't a social call because he'd never visited her in the pink mansion before. They conducted most of their business on the phone.

The director stood up and began pacing the floor. "Just to let you know, I've contacted Sheriff Johnson regarding a cat hoarding situation. The Center only has so

many cages and cannot shelter as many as a hundred cats
—"

"A hundred cats? Where?" Katherine interrupted with concern.

"A woman who lives on County Road 150 West."

"What? Jake and I have rented a farmhouse on that road."

"The woman's name is Elizabeth Howe."

"Elizabeth Howe," Katherine repeated, trying to make a connection between the woman brandishing a shotgun and a suspected hoarder with a hundred cats.

"We have reason to believe she's not taking care of her cats," he continued.

"I beg to differ," Katherine said in a disbelieving voice.

"What do you mean?" he asked, surprised.

"I met her. Her cats were with her. I counted seven cats, or maybe eight, certainly not a hundred."

"As the director, it's my job to take action on what witnesses have complained about."

"Complained? The woman lives out in the middle of nowhere. How did people even get close enough to count the number of cats she has? How did they get past her front gate?"

"That's exactly what I mean. She has a very difficult personality. I have credible, reliable witnesses."

"Who?"

"I'm not at liberty to say right now. I need to protect their privacy, at least until the authorities decide to file charges."

"Charges? Dr. Goodwin, need I remind you that I financed the Center?" Katherine asked, firmly. "And pay your salary. I certainly have the right to know who is making these allegations."

Dr. Goodwin didn't answer but gave a smug look. His cell phone pinged with a text message. "Excuse me. One second, please," he said, then looked at the screen. Melinda had texted. The director moved over to the window to read it. "Mission aborted," she texted. "The witch was home. Cats attacked me. Come get me. Can't drive." The director typed in a return message, "Be there in a few." He sent the message, then looked at Katherine. "I apologize for this. One of the volunteers has a problem."

"Can I do anything to help?"

"No, thanks for asking. I've got it covered."

"Getting back to what we were talking about," Katherine said. "Elizabeth Howe's cats appeared to be in great health. I think you've been duped by the rumor mill that is going around town."

"That she's a witch," he accused, raising his voice. "Frankly, I think she's a witch in more ways than one."

Iris didn't like the angry tone of Dr. Goodwin. She ran to find Jake, but Jake had already entered the room. "Is there a problem?" Jake asked, concerned.

Dr. Goodwin composed himself and said civilly, "It was a problem, but now it's being take care of." He strode toward the front door, opened it, and left.

Iris yowled, frightened. Jake picked her up, cradled her like an infant, and cooed, "It's okay, baby girl."

Katherine said in confused wonderment, "Wow, the Director of the Rescue Center — who I thought was perfect for the job — is hell bent on doing something I totally disagree with."

Jake put Iris down on the floor. "Can you stop him?"

"What I meant to say, it's already been done." She quickly brought Jake up to speed about the director contacting Sheriff Johnson about a cat hoarding accusation.

Jake asked, "Who's the cat hoarder?"

"Professor Howe."

Jake reacted differently from what Katherine expected. He wasn't surprised. Instead, he brought his hand up to his face to cover his mouth to refrain from laughing. "Katz, this is a joke. I've been to Lizzie's house before Nicholas disappeared. She's spotlessly clean, and her cats live the life of Riley."

"Jake, it's not a joke. What if sheriff drives out to talk to her and she shoots him?"

"I don't believe she'd do that. Knowing her, she'll invite the sheriff into her house, show him her cats, which will be a few and not a hundred, and then be done with it. Sheriff Johnson will be annoyed that he wasted his time driving out there."

"Dr. Goodwin called Elizabeth a witch. I didn't expect to hear that from a professional. I guess he's jumped on the bandwagon with a lot of other people in this town."

"The local rumor mill is rife with talk about Professor Howe, and has been for several years now."

"Sounds more like a witch hunt," Katherine commented. The doorbell sounded again. "What is this? Grand Central Station?" she asked, annoyed.

"It has to be my dad," Jake said, sprinting to the door.

Katherine rose from the loveseat and walked over to the wingback chair. She got down on her hands and knees. Iris trotted over and jumped on the seat. She head-butted Katherine's forehead, then peered over the edge.

78

"What did you hide in there, my brown-masked thief?"

"Yowl," Iris answered innocently.

Katherine heard the front door close and assumed Jake was outside on the porch, talking to his dad. She ran her hand inside the torn lining of the chair, and was surprised she didn't find anything.

"I know it was you, Fredo. I saw you steal it from Dr. Goodwin's pocket. Now, where is it?"

Jake came back inside the house and returned to the room. "What are you doing?"

"I thought I saw Iris steal something from the director, but there's nothing in the chair."

"Let me look," Jake said, tipping the chair over on its side. He ran his hand inside the chair. "Didn't find anything, which is odd, because I swore one of the cats stole my toothbrush."

Katherine giggled, then turned to the direction of the door leading to the kitchen. She heard a whishing sound.

Abby proudly entered the room with a blueberry pancake clamped in her teeth. Straddling the rest of the pancake like a spider, the ruddy-colored Abyssinian gingerly clamped her jaw on one edge, while the rest, in all its flapjack glory, grazed the floor.

Jake stood up and laughed.

Katherine ran to Abby. "Gimme that."

Abby paid no attention and slowly continued to the wingback chair.

Katherine leaned down and grabbed the pancake. It tore and landed on the floor. Abby began to eat what was left of it.

The deliberate feline distraction allowed Iris to grab her loot stuck in the fold of the chair cushion and move it to a different site. The seal-point clutched the prize in her jaws and galloped to the kitchen. With feline eyes, she scanned the room for Katherine's purse. When she spotted it lying on the floor next to the refrigerator, she trotted over and dropped the key into the side fold. "Yowl," she cried proudly. She scampered back to the living room.

Jake righted the chair. "Katz, come to the kitchen. There's more batter left. I'll make you another one."

"Okay, that's great because I'm starving right now. Where's your dad?"

"It wasn't him."

"Who was it?"

"Daryl."

"Your cousin Daryl?" she asked, surprised. They hadn't seen Daryl for several months.

Jake nodded. "He's got a problem."

"What?" she asked, with eyes wide open.

"It's not good news."

"Tell me?" she pleaded.

"He broke up with Colleen."

Katherine collapsed on the loveseat. "Oh, no. This is terrible news. Colleen said things weren't right between them. This isn't going to sit well with my friend."

"I know."

"Can't we fix it? Do something to get them back together?"

Jake sadly shook his head.

"Why not?" Katherine questioned, not giving up.

"He kinda hinted he's interested in someone else."

Katherine brought her hand up to her face in shock. "No, I can't believe it. I thought they'd get married, have a truckload of red-headed kids."

"I'm shocked too." Jake walked over and sat down next to Katherine. He took her hand in his. "There's something else. He's asked me to do a big favor for him."

"What is it?"

"I won't be staying with you and our cats the first night at the farmhouse."

"Why not?"

"Daryl needs me to help him drive to Ohio, Tuesday night. He rented a flatbed truck to haul the '67 Chevy Impala to a car show —"

"Why you? Can't he find somebody else?"

"Katz, I promised him, several months ago, if Colleen couldn't do it for this or that other reason, I'd go."

"Jake, promises *can* be broken."

Jake became quiet and gave off a look of dejection. He whispered, "Daryl asked the usual suspects and no one can do it. I promised."

Katherine pouted for a minute, then said, "You said that already. So I take it, the cats and I are to stay at the farmhouse *by ourselves* the first night?"

"Actually it's for two nights."

Katherine didn't answer.

Jake consoled. "Katz, you're a strong woman and very capable of taking care of yourself."

"What's that supposed to mean?" she asked, annoyed.

"Let me put it this way," he began in his professor-like voice. "Back in the day, if you were on a covered wagon trip, heading out west, you'd make it."

Katherine looked at him like he'd lost his mind. "What?"

"You'd make the trip because you're a pioneer."

"What has staying at the farmhouse, *by myself, mind you*," she said with emphasis, "have to do with me being a pioneer?"

"You've got a gun."

Katherine couldn't be angry at Jake for very long. She smiled and gave him a loving look. "That's ridiculous," she said.

Jake put his arm around her. "Here's an idea. Why don't you wait to move until I come back?"

"I can't."

"Why not?"

"The remodel of the attic starts Wednesday. I don't want to mess with the schedule. Margie's got everything orchestrated like clockwork. What time are you leaving Tuesday night?"

"Daryl said sometime after midnight. He'll call me later and let me know the exact time. Why don't you call Colleen and see if she can stay with you a few days."

"How'd you know she'd want to come? She's probably jumping off a bridge right now!"

"It wasn't fair of Daryl to end things the way he did."

"And how was that?"

"He sent her a text."

"A text?" Katherine asked incredulously. "How tacky! Colleen didn't deserve that. For pity sake, she's dated Daryl for a long time. I wonder how his family is going to react. They love her."

"He said he didn't want to talk about it, but I'll try to find out more information on this trip."

"I suppose," Katherine said with a long face.

"Here's an idea. How about I take Scout and Abra to the vet, then drive them out to the farmhouse on my way to Ohio? That way you can get a jump start moving the other cats to the Baxter place."

"Seriously? You're going to drive a flatbed truck down that narrow country road?"

"No, I'm driving the Jeep. Daryl is driving the flatbed."

"Why doesn't Daryl just drive the Impala so the two of you can ride together?"

"He doesn't want to put the mileage on the car. A lot of classic car enthusiasts do this."

"This still doesn't make any sense to me. I thought you were going to help him drive?"

"I meant, Sweet Pea, I'm driving separately behind him in case there's a problem," Jake explained. "Colleen volunteered to do this but now since they've broken up —"

"Hell hath no fury as a woman scorned," Katherine said, shaking her head. "Fury times two."

"What does that mean?"

"You know the stereotype: Irish and red-headed? Look out, Daryl. If you know the name of the woman your cousin ditched my best friend for, don't tell me. Okay?" Katherine's green eyes narrowed in anger.

"I promise."

Jake gathered Katherine into his arms and kissed her on the lips. "I love you, Sweet Pea."

Chapter Six

Dr. Goodwin hurried out of the pink mansion, got in his Mercedes and stomped on the accelerator. He did a U-turn and broke every posted speed limit to race out of town. He had to get to Melinda before she did anything stupid. He worried that her failed attempt at burglary would somehow lead back to him and jeopardize everything he had worked so hard to build. He was more worried about himself than his lover. He feared she'd keep texting him until he answered. He didn't want to go home and have Melinda pinging his cell phone every second. His wife would become suspicious, and start asking questions. He'd have to come up with something fast to cover his tracks.

Turning onto the county road, and driving a few miles to the farmer's service lane, he checked his rear view mirror. A newer gray pickup was following a safe distance behind. The same vehicle had followed him out of Erie. He wondered why and shifted nervously in his seat. Something was sending off a red flag, and he couldn't explain why.

He didn't want anyone to see him driving on this road. He just wanted to park, find Melinda, and take her home. He'd worry about her car another time. She said she'd been attacked by cats, and couldn't drive. He had zero empathy for Melinda's pain and suffering. He didn't want to be inconvenienced by taking her to the hospital, that is, if her injuries were serious. If that was the case, and anyone asked at the hospital, he'd say Melinda was attacked by one of the cats at the Center. That wouldn't raise any eyebrows, except that a smart person would know the Center was closed on Sundays. *I'll just take her to the 24/7 clinic in the City*, he thought, solving that problem.

He was annoyed he hadn't been able to talk Melinda out of her hair-brained scheme. She created such angst for a piece of jewelry. *What if Lizzie Howe called the sheriff?* he fretted. *Melinda, you little fool, you could have been shot by that crazy cat lady.* "And that damn pickup won't get off my ass," he shouted out loud.

He pulled over and stopped near the service lane, powered his window down, and gestured to the driver to drive around.

The driver of the pickup didn't oblige. Instead, the driver drove the truck up behind the Mercedes and parked.

Craning his neck and partially leaning out the window, Dr. Goodwin yelled, "Go around, you freakin' idiot."

The driver of the truck just sat there.

He studied his left side mirror. The pickup driver ducked down as if he was reaching down on the floorboard for something.

"Dammit, go around," the director yelled sounding more anxious than irritated.

The pickup driver switched his headlights from low beam to bright.

Blinded by the glare in the mirror, Dr. Goodwin didn't notice that the driver had gotten out of his truck and was walking up to him.

His instincts told him to step on the accelerator and drive off, but he froze. He couldn't leave Melinda out here with that jerk in the pickup.

Something knocked on the back passenger door behind him. Taking action, he released his seat belt and started to slide across the console to escape through the passenger door, but he was too late.

The pickup driver aimed a handgun at Dr. Goodwin's head and fired one shot. The bullet killed the director instantly. His body slumped against the steering wheel causing the horn to sound. It emitted a deafening blare.

The shooter ran back to his pickup, jumped in, and sped down the road.

Melinda Hudson stood behind a corn row and observed the terrible event. Holding a balled-up paper towel to her injured eye, she ran to assist Dr. Goodwin. Making sure the shooter's vehicle was out-of-sight, she jogged up to the Mercedes. She gently pushed Dr. Goodwin from the steering wheel, which caused the horn to stop. She screamed when she saw the bullet wound in his forehead.

"Oh, no . . . no . . . no, you can't die," she panicked. "What am I going to do?"

She didn't want to be involved in this. She didn't want the town to know she was cheating with a married man. She was a witness and knew the driver. If she blabbed to the sheriff who it was, she was as good as dead. She had to get out of there.

Running back to her car still parked on the service lane, she tripped on a root and fell headlong on her face. The shock knocked the wind out of her. A hand grabbed the back of her navy blue jacket and tugged her up to a sitting position. Turning to see who it was, she screamed again.

A thin man dressed in a scarecrow costume mumbled, "You're going to be okay, but get the hell out of here." He darted into the cornfield and disappeared after the second row.

Dazed by the fall, Melinda slowly picked herself up and leaned against her car. Her head was spinning, and her heart was racing a mile a minute. *What if the shooter comes back? Who the hell was that man wearing scarecrow clothes?* Mustering enough strength to climb into her car, she sat down behind the wheel and locked the doors. She'd lost the paper towel she held against her eye, so she tore off another sheet and pressed it to her eyelid. Abandoning her plan to drive to the hospital, she did something she didn't want to do. She called the sheriff's department. Screaming into her phone, she gave some of the details but left out who did it. She ended the call with "Dr. Goodwin is dead. Hurry up and get here."

Chapter Seven

Later that afternoon, Katherine was on the pink mansion's front porch, decorating one of the front columns with a five-foot scarecrow. She stood high on a step ladder. She was having trouble hooking a bungee cord around the craft store decoration when Stevie Sanders and his daughter Salina walked over from the Foursquare.

"Whatcha doin'?" Stevie asked.

"I'm trying to fasten this scarecrow to the column," Katherine answered, leaning too far. The step ladder swung to the left and started to tip over. Stevie rushed up the steps and righted the ladder.

"You know you ain't good with ladders," he said, recalling the time he had caught Katherine midair when she fell off a high ladder in the carriage house. "Get down from there."

Katherine climbed down. "Thanks. I've got a lot going on this week and falling isn't on my list. Did you just say ain't?"

"What's wrong with that?" he asked sheepishly, brushing a strand of blond hair away from his face.

Katherine rolled her eyes. She'd been working with Stevie to improve his speech.

Salina ran up and hugged Katherine. "I love you, KC." Salina nicknamed Katherine KC because she said Katz sounded too much like cats, and whenever she said it, the Siamese thought she was talking about them.

Katherine hugged her back. Ever since the two of them shared a secret staircase to avoid a Russian hitman they had become thick as thieves.

Stevie joked, "Do I get a hug too?"

Katherine said abruptly, "No."

"I didn't mean you. I meant Salina," Stevie said. "But I wouldn't say no to a hug from you," he added with a wink.

Katherine blushed.

"I'm just messin' with ya. Where's Jake?" he asked.

"He took a load of furniture to the farmhouse we rented."

"By himself?"

"No, his dad helped. He should be back any minute."

"You should have called me. I've been doin' nothin' all day. I could have lent a hand."

"Thanks. Appreciate that."

"Give me that scarecrow," he said, snatching the decoration out of her hands. "I'll fix it for ya." Stevie climbed the ladder and quickly attached the decoration to the column. Stepping back down, he said, "That will cost you a hundred bucks."

"Put it on my tab," she joked.

Salina whined. "KC, I don't want you to move."

"It'll only be for a couple of months. You and your dad can come and visit anytime." Then Katherine pointed to Stevie, "If you've got plans some evening, Salina and Wolfy Joe can stay over. My cats would love it."

Stevie grinned. "You thinkin' I've got a girlfriend?"

"I didn't mean it like that. I meant . . ."

"Yes, you did," he laughed, cutting her off.

Margie, driving Cokey's old Dodge Ram, drove up and parked in front of the mansion. Her daughter, Shelly, was with her and got out of the truck first. Salina ran down the steps to greet them.

Stevie, uncomfortable in Margie's presence because of past history, bowed out and walked back home. Both Margie and Cokey held a grudge against Stevie and were not shy in telling Katherine to watch her back around the ex-con.

Margie got out and yelled up to Katherine. "Hey, Kiddo, I got somethin' for ya." She lowered the truck gate and tugged out a bale of straw. "Girls, can you help me with this?"

Shelly and Salina grabbed a side of the bale and carried it to the porch.

Katherine said to Margie, "I bought nine pumpkins —"

"Goodness, why so many?" Margie interrupted.

"Cause I need to place them on and in front the bale of hay."

Salina pointed at the parlor window. "Look who's watching us."

Shelly greeted, "Hey, Lilac! Hey, Abby!"

The felines stood up on their hind legs and pawed the window glass. Crowie joined them and did the same.

Katherine commented, "That's a rare sight. Usually, they're up high on the window valance."

"KC, can we go in and play with the cats?" Salina asked.

Katherine smiled. "Sure, the cats will love that."

Margie said, "Shelly, come back out in ten minutes, okay? We've got to go to the store and get something to fix for dinner."

"Sure, mom," Shelly said, walking to the front door and opening it. Salina slid in behind her.

Katherine sat down on the bale of hay. "It's pretty comfy. Want to have a sit-down?"

"Don't mind if I do," Margie said, sitting down.

"How's life been treating you?" Katherine asked.

"Pretty good. I've got two more restorations lined up after I finish your project."

"Cool."

"Since you're moving to the Baxter place, why are you decorating the pink mansion?"

"Because it's fun, and Jake and I want people to think we're here and not want to break into the place."

"Good thinking. Cokey and I will keep an eye on the house. I don't think you have anything to worry about. Besides, I'll be working here during the day. When I pack up to leave, I'll arm the security system."

"I really appreciate it. You never know with the pink mansion. It's starting to be the season when tourists walk up and down the historic district, taking pictures of the old houses. Since my house has been named the murder house —"

"Oh, hog wash, the locals don't call it that. They still call it the Colfax mansion."

"Out-of-towners are curious about the mansion because of the negative publicity. The house has been such a murder magnet. I don't want lookie loos vandalizing the place while we're gone."

"Vandalize? Why would you think someone would vandalize it?"

"Something that happened yesterday," Katherine answered pensively.

"Geez, you've got me curious. What happened?"

"When Colleen and I drove out to the farmhouse, we passed this property with a rusted mailbox attached to an equally rusted farm gate—"

Margie cut Katherine off. "Sounds like a lot of properties out that way. Folks are either too busy to replace their junk mailboxes or sick of the local hooligans knocking them down."

"Knock them down? Why?"

"It's a teenager thing. Like a rite of passage. They pile into a car or truck, drive around the country, and use a ball bat to knock down mailboxes."

"For an ex-New Yorker, I find this hard to believe."

"Yep. Stuff happens, but go back to this rusted gate. I didn't mean to interrupt."

"It wasn't the rusted mailbox or gate that got my attention. It was more of what was at the gate."

Margie gestured with her hand. "And?"

"The gate had witch symbols plastered all over it."

Margie put her hand to her throat and feigned surprise. "Please, tell me you didn't stop there."

"You know about this place?"

"Everyone in town knows about the crazy woman who lives there. She's nuttier than a fruitcake."

"You mean Elizabeth Howe?"

"Yes, but people around here call her Lizzie the lunatic."

"That's not a very nice nickname," Katherine disapproved. "Jake said she's well-educated, taught at the university until she took early retirement. He said she's a bit eccentric, but not crazy. How do you know her?"

"She sells candles and handmade soap at the flea market in Millbridge. She dresses up like a witch and sells soap called 'Witch Soap.'"

Katherine giggled. "Is it any good?"

Margie winked. "Oh hell yes. It's the best soap *ever*."

"Sounds likes she's got a good gimmick to attract customers."

Margie added, "She always has a big black cat sitting on her table. The cat isn't very friendly, and would rather bite you than let you pet it."

"Why would that make her crazy?"

"There's talk around town that she murdered her husband, Nicholas."

"Jake said that was a vicious rumor. How can she be accused of murdering her husband when his body was never found?"

Margie shrugged. "Don't know the answer to that."

"Maybe Nicholas left her and moved to another state. He could be in Hawaii right now drinking a Mai-tai."

"Lizzie had an affair with Nicholas who was married to Melinda."

"Melinda who?"

"Melinda Howe, I mean Melinda Hudson. She took her maiden name back after the divorce. You know her, don't you? She volunteers at your rescue center."

"I've run into her a few times. She seems pretty tough. I wouldn't want to tangle with her, and I certainly wouldn't want her to catch me having an affair with her husband."

"Me either," Margie agreed. "Lizzie broke up the marriage. Nicholas divorced Melinda, Nicholas married Lizzie and Lizzie killed him. That's what everyone in town says."

"You mean everyone in town or everyone at the diner?"

"No, I mean ninety-nine percent of the people in Erie think she murdered Nicholas and buried him on her land."

"Who started this rumor? The ex-wife?"

"Well, I don't know exactly. Melinda Hudson wasn't happy. She has a short fuse. We were afraid she'd take the law into her own hands and murder Lizzie. She threatened to and was put in jail to cool down. The case was investigated, but Sheriff Johnson never solved it."

"When did this happen?"

"Before you moved here. Four years ago, I think." Margie cleared her throat, then asked. "So what happened when you stopped at her gate? Did Lizzie run out with a shotgun?"

"How'd you know?"

"A little birdie told me."

"Is he over six feet tall and lives with me at the pink mansion?"

"You got it. Jake told Cokey who told me. You're lucky Lizzie didn't shoot you."

"After what Jake has told me about her, I don't think she would have shot us."

"Did he tell you she used to volunteer at the old animal shelter, and when the time came to put down a cat —"

"You mean to put to sleep? I hate the E-word."

"I don't like it either. Whenever a cat hadn't been adopted, after a certain amount of time, or the shelter was full . . . whenever that happened, Lizzie would freak out and throw such a hissy fit, the shelter folks would let her take the cat."

"How many times did this happen?"

"I heard quite a few times."

"Wasn't this kind of in-house rescue against the shelter's rules?"

"Hey, Kiddo, seriously? By letting Lizzie have the cat, the shelter didn't have to put it to sleep. It made for happy employees who'd rather see Lizzie take the poor creature than having to do the deed."

"It sounds like Lizzie has an emotional problem —"

"Or a big heart. Depends on how you look at it."

"I'm so happy I stepped into the picture and funded the no-kill center."

"You've paved your way to Heaven, I'm sure."

Katherine smiled, then returned to the subject. "I'm surprised no one at the Center has told me about Lizzie."

"Probably because Melinda is thick with everyone that works there, and they don't want to upset her by mentioning the woman who stole her husband."

"Four years is a long time to be harboring a grudge. I take it Melinda didn't remarry or find someone else."

"Nope, she said Nicholas was the love of her life. Here's something you don't know. Several months after you appointed Dr. Goodwin as the new director, Lizzie quit. She said that she'd rather be stabbed by an ice pick then be in the same room with him."

Katherine scrunched her face in disgust. "Oh, yuk. What a visual. Why doesn't she like Dr. Goodwin?"

"She told a friend of mine, that Dr. Goodwin made a pass at her on multiple occasions."

Katherine covered her mouth with one hand to refrain from laughing.

"What's so funny?"

"Margie, Dr. Goodwin is the homeliest man I've ever met. I couldn't imagine him doing anything so harassing."

"Some women find ugly sexy."

"But he's married."

"That doesn't stop some men around here or some women. Lizzie is a local gal. She's led a tragic life. Her first husband committed suicide; her second one took off with a married woman who was a maid at the Erie Hotel. Then, she decided to mess with Melinda's husband."

"Wow, this sounds like a soap opera."

"I don't know how Nicholas did it, but he convinced Melinda to move out and then Lizzie moved in."

"Wait, hang on a second. You're saying that Nicholas owns the land Lizzie lives on?"

"Yep, the Howe farmstead has been around for over a century. Nicholas retitled the property in his name and hers after they married. One of my drywall guys said some rich developers want to buy it."

"Why? How would they even know about it? It's out in the sticks."

"It's close to the interstate."

"What does that mean?" Katherine asked.

"It means it's close to an exit and would make an ideal place for a gas station, fast-food restaurant, or even a mini-grocery store."

Katherine reached over and tapped Margie on the arm. "Hey, thanks for the intel."

"No problem."

Chief London drove his Erie town police cruiser in front of the mansion and parked behind Margie's truck. He got out, adjusted his black police ball cap, and walked up the steps. "Good afternoon, ladies," he said with a wide grin.

"I'd offer you a seat," Katherine said, patting the bale of hay, "but they're all taken."

"Thank you kindly, but I've been sittin' on my behind all day, plastered in front of the TV, watchin' movies on demand. I'll just lean against the railing."

Margie blurted, "Did Katz tell ya about that crazy Lizzie Howe woman pointing a gun at her?"

The chief looked at Katherine and gave a conspiratorial wink.

"Guilty," Katherine said, putting her hands up. "I'm a bonafide trespasser."

The chief chuckled, then became serious. "Sheriff Johnson called me yesterday. I meant to stop by, but got tied up with something else."

Katherine began, "I called the sheriff's department and told dispatch what happened. I kind of expected the sheriff would give me a call. What did he say?"

"He said he's up to his ears with complaints about Elizabeth Howe."

"You mean I'm not the only one she's pointed a gun at?"

"Among other things."

"Colleen and I didn't mean to trespass."

"I know that, but Elizabeth Howe didn't. Anyway, Sheriff Johnson drove out there and checked it out. Elizabeth met him at the gate."

"Does she hang out at her gate all the time?" Katherine asked.

"She's got a wireless driveway alarm connected to her house. Whenever someone approaches, a chime sounds inside. That gives her a few minutes to walk to the gate to see who's there."

"Did she have her shotgun?" Margie asked, tongue-in-cheek.

"No, not this time. The sheriff said she apologized for her behavior, but she's at her wit's end to find out who is vandalizing her gate with supernatural —"

"Witch symbols," Katherine finished.

"We want to hear more," Margie probed, adjusting her seat on the bale.

"Basically, Sheriff Johnson said it's malicious mischief. He thinks it's a bunch of kids playing games, but what he doesn't want to happen is for one of the kids to get shot."

Katz asked naively, "You think children put those witch symbols there?"

The chief took his cap off and scratched his head. Repositioning it, he said, "I meant teenagers. The sheriff said he saw lots of footprints, cigarette butts and some beer cans."

"But why would a bunch of teenagers target a woman living out in a rural area?"

"This I don't know, but the sheriff and one of his deputies picked up the debris the best they could. He suggested to Ms. Howe that she install a security camera. He even said there's a convenient telephone pole near her entrance."

Katherine nodded, "If I lived out there by myself, I'd definitely have a security camera."

"Sheriff Johnson is stepping up patrols past her house to find out who's doing this. When I mentioned that

Jake and you are moving out that way, he said he might even stop by and introduce himself."

"Tuesday is moving day," Katherine said cheerfully.

"I heard it this morning at the diner. Went in for a cup of coffee, and the place was hoppin' with information, misinformation, and downright gossip."

Katherine was amazed at the communication network in the small town. Everyone knew everyone else's business.

Margie laughed, but Katherine thought, *Sometimes I wish people would mind their own business.*

"Question to you, Katz? Will the monthly meeting be here or at the Baxter farmhouse?"

"Let's have it at the farmhouse. I'll text the two of you the date and time."

"That settles that," the chief said, then added, "I've got to go home before the wife has a canary. She doesn't like it when I'm late for dinner."

Margie said, "Chief, you're pulling our leg. Connie is the wife of a police chief. I'm sure your official police business has interrupted dinner quite a few times."

"You got it!" He tipped his cap, then looked at Katherine. "Katz, could I have a private word with you. No offense, Margie."

Margie pursed her lips. "None taken."

"Of course," Katherine said, getting up.

"Walk me to my car," the chief suggested.

When they got to the cruiser, the chief's cell rang. "Just a second, Katz." He answered the call, spoke for a moment, then hung up. "There's more to the Elizabeth Howe story," he said in a low voice.

"What?"

"What I'm about to tell you is for your ears only."

"Understood." Katherine imitated zipping her lip.

"I'm sorry to be the bearer of bad news, but you're going to have to hire a new director for your rescue center."

"Why?" Katherine gasped, fearing bad news.

"Dr. Goodwin is dead."

"Dead?" Katherine asked, shocked. "He can't be. He was just over here this morning."

"He was found shot in his car."

"Where? At the Center?"

"In front of Elizabeth Howe's property."

"Oh, my god! She shot him?"

"I don't know the answer to that. The case is being investigated by Sheriff Johnson. By the way, what was Dr. Goodwin's mood when you saw him?"

"He went from being pleasant to biting my head off. He accused Elizabeth Howe of cat hoarding, and he was adamant to go to the prosecutor for a warrant."

"Interesting."

"But during our conversation he was interrupted by a text message."

"From who?"

"He said one of the Center's volunteers had a problem. When I offered to help, he said he had it under control."

"Do any of the volunteers have it out for Dr. Goodwin?"

"No, not that I know of. Margie said that Elizabeth Howe was a volunteer and quit because Dr. Goodwin made a pass at her. She said that Lizzie despised him."

"Okay, then, I think the sheriff should know about the text message. It's possible that it could be the last message Dr. Goodwin read before he was murdered. Maybe the person that sent the message was the one who shot him. I'll pass that info on to the sheriff as well as what Margie said about Elizabeth. Also, I have more bad news."

"How could it get any worse?"

The chief glanced over at the Foursquare. "Salina's grandmother is in town. She's been spouting some pretty defamatory remarks about Stevie at the Erie Hotel restaurant."

"What's she doing in Erie? I thought she lived in Kentucky."

"Seems she's here on business, but she's also saying she wants custody of Salina."

Katherine's jaw dropped in shock. "No, she can't take Salina. If half of what I've heard is true, the woman is a crim."

"You're right about her being a criminal, but she hasn't broken any Indiana laws. Just thought you should know she's in town. In the event something goes south, can you make sure Salina is okay?"

"Yes, by all means. It bogles my mind, that she'd want to take Salina away from her dad. Stevie has gone clean. He's a very good father. Besides, I haven't had a chance to tell you, but Jake and I are Salina's legal standby guardians. We signed the documents at the courthouse."

"You're a good soul. Now, excuse me, been a long day doin' nothin', I'm headin' home."

"Okay, chief. Thanks for stopping by."

"Oh, turn on your TV. I'm sure Dr. Goodwin's murder will make the five o'clock news."

"Yes, thanks." Katherine frowned, waited for the chief to get in his cruiser and drive away before she joined Margie back on the porch. She was worried — very worried. Salina's grandmother was a criminal, so was Stevie's dad.

Poor Salina. What a pair of grandparents she had, Katherine thought. The last person on earth she wanted Salina to live with was her criminal grandmother. She considered Stevie her friend. She wanted to warn him, but couldn't. If she did, and the chief found out, he'd never divulge information to her again. She relied on the chief's friendship as well.

And, now Dr. Goodwin was dead — murdered close to the farmhouse where Jake, she, and the cats would be staying for two months. Whoever killed him was at large. *I'm not going to feel safe living out there until the murderer is caught,* she worried.

Chapter Eight

Melinda Hudson sat on a gurney inside an Erie County ambulance. An EMT had placed a gauze pad over her left eye and taped it to her cheek and forehead. She lightly tapped it with her hand and asked, "Am I goin' lose my sight in that eye?"

The EMT answered, "No, Ma'am. Your eye wasn't scratched but you've got quite a gash on your upper eyelid. I've stopped the bleeding for now, but we're going to take you to the hospital so they can check you out. They might want to put in sutures."

"You mean stitches?" she cried, dabbing the tears flowing from her right eye. "Can't you do that right now?"

"I applied three butterfly stitches, but they're temporary."

Melinda continued to cry in frustration, and deep grief in losing the only man in her life since Nicholas.

"I know it hurts, but Ma'am, stop crying. Your tears might make the wound start bleeding again."

Looking out her right eye, she saw flashing lights through the corn plants. She assumed it was the sheriff and deputies investigating the scene.

"Am I going to have a scar?" she asked, returning to the topic of her injury.

The EMT empathized, "I'm sorry. I really can't answer that. You might want to go to a plastic surgeon and discuss that with him."

"Plastic surgeon!" she shrieked. "I'm not paying for that! That witch Lizzie is goin' to. It was her cats that scratched me."

A large black cat jumped up onto the tailgate. "Roooahh," the cat cried.

"Get out of here," the EMT yelled at the cat.

The black cat didn't move and answered with a hiss.

Melinda screamed. "Get that animal away from me."

Lizzie hurried up to the back of the ambulance and said to the cat, "Go home, Amara. Take the other cats and go home."

Amara meowed and jumped down.

Lizzie moved closer to Melinda and threatened. "My cats didn't attack you. Stay away from my property."

"You freakin' witch. I'm going to sue you!"

"Now ladies," the EMT said, holding Melinda's arm so she couldn't get up.

One of the deputies heard the altercation and came over. "Is there a problem here?" he asked.

The EMT pointed at Lizzie. "Can you take this woman away from here?"

The deputy put his hand on Lizzie's arm. She shrugged it off. "I'm leaving." Adjusting her shawl over her sundress, she walked back to her farm gate.

Melinda said to the deputy, "Look, Sir, I've been detained long enough. The sheriff can ask me questions at the hospital. I demand to go to the hospital NOW."

Sheriff Johnson was standing nearby, talking to the coroner. He was ruggedly handsome — a dead ringer for the movie actor Ed Harris. When he heard Melinda, an annoyed expression swept over his face. He walked over to the ambulance.

"Ms. Hudson, you'll stay here until I say you can leave. Got that?"

"My eye hurts."

"I'm sorry. I assure you I only need to ask you a few more questions. I want you to rethink what you told me earlier about the shooter."

"Are you trying to make me recant my statement?" she accused belligerently.

"You need to get something straight. You need to cooperate. If you weren't injured, I'd haul you off to jail in a second."

"Better show some respect," the EMT advised Melinda.

Melinda started to say something, then thought twice. "I'll tell you again, but the next time, I want my attorney present."

The sheriff began, "Why were you parked in the Baxters' service lane?"

"Dr. Goodwin called and asked me to meet him here. He wanted me to come with him when he talked to Lizzie about her hoarding cats."

"Do you work for Dr. Goodwin . . . I mean the late Dr. Goodwin?"

"I'm a volunteer down at the Center. He thought I should come along because I once lived in Lizzie's house when I was married to Nicholas."

The sheriff was quiet for a few seconds, and didn't reveal that he'd already checked out the hoarding situation and that Lizzie was not collecting cats. Lizzie had eight cats, all of which were fine and up-to-date with their vaccinations. Lizzie was definitely not a hoarder. He wanted to get to the bottom of why Melinda was saying otherwise.

Melinda blurted, "I was early, so I got out of my car. That's when Lizzie's cats attacked me."

The EMT interrupted, "Ma'am, I don't believe your wound was inflicted by an animal, cat or otherwise. Your gash is too deep."

"Were you there? Did you see it happen? I'm tellin' ya I got attacked by cats," she said defiantly.

The sheriff said knowingly, "Melinda, you're wearing a navy blue jacket. I found a piece of material snagged on the barbed-wire fence in front of Elizabeth Howe's property. Care to explain how you've got a torn piece on your jacket that matches that material?"

Melinda was momentarily speechless. Looking down at her torn jacket, she said, "Purely coincidental."

The EMT continued, "Her wound was probably caused by falling on the barbed-wire. I'll make sure the hospital staff administers a Tetanus shot."

The sheriff answered, "Good idea," then to Melinda, "Tell me again about the shooter."

"He wore a mask over his face," she said, not establishing eye contact. "It was a hood with the eyes cut out. He wore scarecrow clothes. You know . . . plaid shirt, bib overalls. He's a tall, skinny dude well over six feet tall," she answered in a dull, monotone voice.

The sheriff looked up at the sky in disbelief. "We found you sitting in your vehicle with a row of corn in front of you. How did you see the shooter with one eye?"

"When I heard the shot, I rushed over to Tony's . . . I mean Dr. Goodwin's . . . car and found him dead."

"So you did or didn't see this scarecrow man shoot him?"

Melinda backtracked and carefully chose her answer. "Sheriff, you're right. I didn't see the scarecrow shoot him. I heard Lizzie Howe bewitch the scarecrow —"

"What does that mean?" the sheriff interrupted, getting irritated at the bogus answers Melinda was giving to his line of questioning.

"She said some sort of witch incantation."

"What's that? Something like Samantha would say on *Bewitched*?"

"Yes, I guess."

"What did you hear Lizzie say?"

"Let me think . . . something like 'by the magic of my black cats, this man holds me back, Scarecrow, set things right.' Then I heard the scarecrow shoot Tony."

"But you didn't see him actually do it."

"When I heard the shot, I ran back to my car and tripped on a root. The scarecrow ran behind me, yanked me up, then fled into the cornfield."

"Why would he set you up?"

"I don't know. I was too terrified to ask him."

"Was he carrying a gun?"

"If he was, I didn't see one."

"And, why was that?"

Melinda thought fast on her feet. "Because he had big tufts of straw sticking out of his cuffs."

The sheriff shook his head and said to the EMT, "That'll be all. Pack it up and take her to the hospital. Make sure they check her for signs of a concussion." He then muttered under his breath, "Lights are on but nobody's home."

Chapter Nine

Katherine stood on the sidewalk, in front of the pink mansion, and waved at Chief London as he pulled out of his parking space. She watched him drive up Lincoln Street until he turned left and was obscured by the brick Italianate on the corner. She hesitated to rejoin Margie on the front porch because her mood had taken a noticeable nose dive from happy to doom-and-gloom. She wanted to compose herself before she faced Margie, who'd pick up on her mood swing and ask a million questions.

Margie picked up the change of mood anyway and asked, "Everything okay?"

"Yes, I hope so."

"Anything I can do?"

"I'm good, thanks."

"Okay, Kiddo," Margie said, getting up. "If you need me, you know where to find me." She reached in her purse for her cell phone. "I've got to text my daughter and tell her to come out here."

As if on cue, Shelly appeared at the parlor window holding Dewey. She cradled the Siamese in her arms, and was rocking him. Salina held Crowie in the same fashion.

Margie motioned her daughter to come outside. Shelly set down the affectionate Siamese and came out, shadowed by Salina.

Margie said, "Well, Katz, gotta run. Shelly are you ready?"

"Yes, mom."

"Kiddo, catch you later."

"Bye," Katherine waved, then patted the recently vacated seat on the hay bale. "Salina, can you sit down for a minute?"

"Yes, ma'am," Salina said, "but I promised Dad I'd fix him his favorite for supper."

Katherine smiled. "What's that?"

"Homemade mac and cheese with bits of green pepper and tomato in it."

"It sounds delicious. I won't keep you long."

Salina sat down and began twisting her long braid.

"In case you need me, you've got my cell number," Katherine began. "Text me whenever you want. I'll be driving back and forth from the farmhouse to the mansion because I'm still teaching my computer class in the afternoon."

"Will you be here every day?"

"Just Tuesdays and Thursdays, but not this Tuesday. I'm moving to the farmhouse then."

"Cool. Maybe Dad can bring me out this weekend or I can ride my bike. I know how to get there," Salina said with a knowing grin. "Wanna know how I know?"

"It's too far for you to ride your bike," Katherine advised. "Have you been at the farmhouse before?"

"No, but I've been to the magic lady's cabin across the road."

"The magic lady? Elizabeth Howe?"

"Uh-huh, but she likes to be called Lizzie."

"Yes, I know. Why is she a magic lady?"

"Because she rescues stray cats and makes them better."

"Interesting. Tell me more."

"She rescued Wolfy Joe. He was all banged up and sick, and she made him okay. That's how I got him."

"Small world," Katherine pondered the interconnections of people in the town, and now the country. "Was Wolfy Joe up for adoption at the old animal shelter?" she questioned.

"Uh-huh. Lizzie told my mom that nobody wanted him because of his age. Mom knew I wanted a cat, so one day I came home from school and Mom drove me to Lizzie's. Lizzie had all these cats in her front room. At first it was hard to choose, then Wolfy came over and gave me the biggest head-butt. It was love at first sight."

"Ahhh," Katherine answered. She wanted to ask more about the so-called witch, now "magic lady," but Salina got up and started to leave.

"Gotta go. Bye, KC," Salina said with a twinkle in her eye. She walked briskly to the Foursquare.

Katherine turned on the bale of hay and watched Salina until she had let herself in the house. She wondered if Wolfy Joe was one of those shelter cats on death row that Lizzie took home to nurse back to health. If so, that wasn't an act a wicked witch would do. *That was done out of love and kindness*, she thought.

Katherine sat for a minute until her reverie was interrupted by the sound of drumming on the nearby turret-glass window. She turned to see which one of her cats was trying to get her attention. Scout and Abra were sitting on the sill. Scout was frantically drumming the glass with her front paws.

"What's wrong?" Katherine said, hurriedly getting off the bale and moving closer to the window.

Scout started swaying. Her pupils were mere slits in her deep blue eyes. Scout arched her back and began hopping up and down. Abra joined the dance and was salivating. Katherine could hear the muffled sound of Siamese shrieks.

Katherine knew the Siamese death dance was never a good sign. The hair raised on the back of her neck. She wondered who the premonition was for; Margie, Shelly,

Stevie or Salina, and wished the cats could be more specific. If it was for Dr. Goodwin, the cats were too late to warn him. She shuddered at the thought and rushed inside to calm down the sensitive felines.

Chapter Ten

Tuesday Afternoon

Katherine and Jake placed five of the cats in two cat carriers and loaded them into the back of the Subaru. While the couple was herding the felines, Scout and Abra made themselves scarce for fear they were going into a dreaded cat carrier as well.

Inside the first carrier, Iris sat on her haunches and washed Dewey's ears while he belted a loud Siamese song that didn't sound anything like "We are Siamese" from *Lady and the Tramp*, but more like the deep baritone of an opera singer. Abby, Crowie and Lilac shared the second carrier. Katherine wanted to put Crowie in a third carrier, but he kept jumping in with Lilac and Abby, so she relented. Lilac me-yowled loudly, but Abby chirped happily and Crowie meowed softly, which was unusual for a Siamese.

Jake used the shoulder belts to fasten the two carriers to the back seat. "Katz, the vet appointment isn't until two hours. I can drive behind you and help you carry them inside the farmhouse, then come back to take Scout and Abra to their appointment."

"That's too much, Jake. Last night, you were up until the wee hours grading papers and you'll be driving to Ohio tonight. I want you to take a nap before you take them. You look exhausted."

"Seriously, Katz, I can help," he offered a second time, yawning.

"Aw, that's sweet, but I want you to rest. I'm anxious to get the show on the road and have the cats comfortable in their cat room at the farmhouse before it gets dark."

"Are you sure you can handle carrying them inside?"

Katherine gave Jake a side glance, "Why Jake, I'm a pioneer woman, remember? You said so yourself."

He laughed, then hugged her. "Okay, text me when you get there."

"I will," she said, climbing in the driver's seat.

"Oh, the weather channel predicted rain," he added.

"Thanks, you just jinxed it."

A clap of thunder startled them. The rain started to pour. Jake tugged his jacket over his head and jogged back to the mansion. Katherine laughed, and turned on the windshield wipers.

"Me-yowl," Lilac cried, frightened by the thunder.

"It's okay, sweet girl."

"Boom," a second crack of thunder sounded, directly overhead. The other cats started caterwauling.

"Calm down, my treasures," Katherine reassured. "I promise it won't take me long to drive to our new place. We're only going to be there for a few months. We've already made sure your favorite cat stuff is there."

"Chirp," Abby approved.

Taking the back route from the mansion, Katherine drove down the narrow alley and then turned onto the main highway. In a soothing voice, she said to the cats, "You guys must be tired. Why don't you curl up and go to sleep?" *Fat chance*, she thought, *I'm sure Lilac will me-yowl the entire trip,* but was pleasantly surprised when the cats did exactly what she asked. Only Lilac put up a fuss but quieted after a few minutes.

Driving onto County Road 150 West, she was passed by a deputy's cruiser. The vehicle was travelling so fast, she couldn't tell if he or she were alone or had someone with them. "What's the hurry?" she asked out loud. She was thankful the rain kept the gravel dust at bay but didn't relish carrying the cat carriers inside the house. She knew she'd get soaked.

Katherine slowed down before Lizzie's farm gate and noticed the pentagram signs had been taken down. A beat-up green Land Rover was parked outside. *Lizzie's*, she surmised.

Looking to the right, she saw the police crime scene tape surrounding the site where Dr. Goodwin was shot. She wished Jake had told her how close it was to the farmhouse entrance. Seeing the tape in person, brought home the fact that the killer was still out there. *Just my luck, he's inside the house ready to kill us all,* she worried, imagining all sorts of scary scenarios. *Maybe I should have taken Jake up on his offer to drive behind us.*

Driving down the farmhouse's lane, Katherine was surprised the deputy's vehicle was parked in front of the house. She parked beside it, grabbed her umbrella and got out. The deputy did also. He walked over to the Subaru. "I thought you might need some help," Jake's blond-haired, green-eyed cousin said.

"Daryl?" she asked, surprised.

"Hello, Katz. Jake called and asked me to help you with the cats."

"That was thoughtful," she said thankfully, but in a cold voice. She still hadn't been able to get past the idea that Daryl had broken up with Colleen with a text message.

"I also wanted to talk to you about Colleen."

"Ah, Daryl, perhaps you should talk to Colleen."

"She won't answer my calls."

"Did you try texting?" she asked with a slightly snide tone.

Daryl gave a curious look. "Yes, but she's not answering my texts either."

Katherine didn't want to discuss her best friend's boyfriend's woes, especially standing outside, getting drenched, in a thunderstorm. She hastily changed the subject. "I'll unlock the door, then come back. You can grab a carrier and follow me."

Katherine ran to the house and up the steps. Extracting the front door key from the fold in her purse, she inserted it in the lock, and it wouldn't turn. "What the hell?" she complained, struggling to once again unlock the door. "Dammit," she cursed.

Daryl came up on the porch with Abby, Lilac, and Crowie. He set the carrier down close to the door. "What's wrong?"

"The door won't open."

"Here, hand me the key and let me try."

Katherine gave him an insolent look and thought, *I just tried and it didn't work.*

Daryl jiggled the key in the lock but couldn't get the door to open either. "Is this the right key?" he asked abruptly.

"Of course it is," Katherine answered, then paused. "Wait a minute," she said, thinking out loud. "My key's on my key ring. What's wrong with me?" She fished her key ring out of her pocket, inserted the antique key in the lock, and the door opened.

That's odd. Where did this extra key come from? she asked herself.

Daryl picked up the carrier and placed it inside. "Katz, you stay here. I'll go fetch the other one."

He ran to the SUV, extracted the carrier, and hurried back. A bolt of lightning hit nearby. The smell of ozone filled the air.

Katherine cringed at the thought of Daryl and the cats being struck by lightning. "Hurry," she called.

Daryl rushed in. "That was a close one," he said. Setting the carrier down, he asked, "If you don't mind, I'll search the house before you come in."

"Please. That would be helpful. I'm a bit nervous with the killer of Dr. Goodwin still out there."

Daryl, dressed in his Brook County Deputy uniform, walked from room to room on both floors. When he returned, he said, "Coast is clear. I also checked under the beds and in the closets. What's in that room with the deadbolt on it?"

"It's the owner's storage room."

"Want me to check it?"

"No, thanks. It's locked to keep one of our cats out."

"I can guess which one," Daryl commented. "Scout, right?"

Katherine nodded, then asked, "I didn't realize you were working today."

"Why's that?"

"Because of the Ohio trip tonight."

"I just got off duty. I was headin' home when Jake called. I must confess I had another motive for seeing you today."

"Does it involve a red-headed Irish gal?"

"I was hoping she'd be here."

"She's coming later. Want me to give her a message?"

"I miss her," he said sadly.

Katherine bit her lip and didn't say what she was thinking, which was why did you break up with her in the first place. Instead, she said, "I'm sure she misses you too, Daryl. I know it's none of my business, but I thought the two of you were meant for each other."

"It's complicated," he said. "Well, I'll be off. I've got a million things to do before Jake and I leave tonight. Catch you later, Katz. Take care." Daryl walked out the front door without looking back. He ran to his cruiser, then left.

Iris yowled impatiently inside the carrier.

"I know sweetie. Let me text Jake that we're here."

She quickly keyed in a message, and then the phone rang. Seeing Jake's name on the screen, she answered, "Did you get dried off?"

"Katz, I'm so glad you made it. Daryl said he was going to meet you there."

"Yes, he was just here and left."

"There's a snag in our plan. After the vet appointment, I have to come back to the mansion. The driver of the drywall truck called and said he's delivering at six."

"What? It's not supposed to arrive until tomorrow. Can't Margie take care of it?"

"I'm afraid not. Cokey said she went to the City to pick up supplies."

"This isn't good. Jake, do me a favor when the construction guys carry in the drywall, please make sure Scout and Abra are locked up in their playroom."

"Sweet Pea, I've got it under control."

"Sorry, I worry too much about our cats. So, when are you bringing Scout and Abra to the farmhouse?"

"It's back to the original plan. When Daryl and I leave for Ohio, he'll drive to the first rest stop on the interstate and wait for me there. I'll make a detour to the farmhouse and drop them off, then catch up with Daryl a little later."

"What time will that be?"

Iris yowled again, this time impatiently.

"Late. I'll text you first."

"Alright then. I'll be here, and probably up. Colleen is coming later. Girls night. Lots to talk about."

Jake joked, "Like how she's going to murder Daryl."

"Something like that. Catch you later. Love you."

"Love you too."

Chapter Eleven

Stevie Sanders drove his red Dodge Ram onto a service road next to an abandoned concrete grain elevator. He drove up and parked behind his dad's metallic gray Toyota Tundra. He wondered why his father chose such an isolated place to meet him. At first he'd declined, suspicious of his dad, but out of curiosity, shrugged off the notion that Sam Sanders would ever harm one of his own sons. It was a known fact that father and son didn't see eye-to-eye on a multitude of things, such as cooking and selling meth or running prostitution rings throughout north central Indiana. But since Salina had entered the picture, dear old Dad was trying to be a good grandfather by keeping a close eye on where they lived and preventing bad things from happening to them.

After prison, Stevie made a few bad choices. He regretted his father getting him involved with drug running, but he'd put a stop to that. He was clean now, and making decent money in his electrical business. He'd served his time for armed robbery and was on parole, so he minded his Ps and Qs. Besides, he had sole custody of his daughter. She meant the world to him. Someone else meant the world to him, but she must never know. He valued Katherine's friendship too much to jeopardize it with a slip of the tongue or a cupid's arrow.

Stevie left the engine and the lights on. He walked up to the Toyota's cab and found it was empty. "Hey, Dad, where are you?" he called, swatting at a mosquito that buzzed his head.

Sam walked out from behind a concrete barrier. He was dressed in a crisp navy blue suit, with a white shirt. His designer loafers were buffed to a high sheen. "Glad you could make it," he greeted, then reached in his pocket.

Stevie stepped back, worried that his dad might be pulling out a gun.

"Want a smoke?" Sam said, holding out a wrapped Cuban cigar.

Relieved that it was a cigar and not a gun, Stevie declined. "No, I quit smokin'."

Sam put it back in his pocket, then lit up his own. "Sorry about your luck. You're missing a great smoke."

"Not interested," Stevie said impatiently. "So what's up? Why did you ask me to meet you, at ten o'clock at night, in this god-forsaken place?"

"I have good news for you."

Stevie gestured with his hands in the air. "What?" he probed.

"I've met a woman online, and asked her to marry me."

Stevie's facial expression went from doubt to amusement. He laughed. "Online? Where's she from?"

"She's an Erie gal, but has spent most of her time in the city."

"What happened to that woman in Chicago?"

"Nothing happened to her. She's still around. What's wrong with having more than one woman in your life?" he answered haughtily.

Stevie shook his head in revulsion. "Have you ever tried monogamy?"

"Nope, can't say I have."

"Why are you so dressed up?" Stevie asked, changing the topic.

"Every woman likes a sharp-dressed man. Haven't you heard the song?"

"What's so special about the new woman?" Stevie gave a skeptical look. "Have you told her you've been married four times and have a son by each wife?"

"We haven't gotten to that part . . . yet."

The singing of the night cicadas reached a deafening crescendo. Stevie swatted another mosquito that landed on his arm. "Who's the lucky lady?"

"Her name is Elizabeth Howe."

"Elizabeth Howe," Stevie pondered, then asked, shocked. "You mean Lizzie the crazy cat lady? She's not exactly your type."

"She's not a crazy cat lady," Sam said indignantly. "That's a damn lie."

"What do you see in her? Isn't she nuts?"

"How would you know?"

"People in town are calling her a witch. They say she uses her black cats to cast spells on folks she doesn't like."

"I guess I better not piss her off," Sam smirked, then added, "You don't believe in that witchcraft crap, do you?"

"No, I don't, but most of the town does. They want to ride her out of town on a rail."

"She's already out-of-town," Sam said sarcastically.

"I mean out of the state of Indiana."

"I'm not going to let that happen. Elizabeth is a beautiful woman and I enjoy her company."

"I thought you just chatted online?"

"I've just spent part of the night with her, and trust me, we didn't chat."

"Enough," Stevie put up his hand in the stop gesture. "I've got to get back home. I don't like leaving Salina alone at night."

"Oh, you worry too much. She'll be okay."

"You don't know that, Dad. I thought you had some kind of crucial business. Instead, you drag me out here so you could talk about your love life," Stevie said, frustrated. He started to walk back to his truck.

"No, you idiot, I had you meet me here because I think I'm being bugged."

"Bugged?"

"Yeah, like by the law. Surveillance."

"If you're carrying your cell phone, the feds know your exact location."

"I'm not stupid. I keep switching burner phones."

"I don't think you lured me out here to talk about Lizzie Howe," Stevie said suspiciously. "You want me to do something for ya, right? Something against the law? That's your MO. You don't give a crap that your son's still on probation. Gee, thank you very much, Pop!" Stevie's face reddened in anger.

"Wait. One second. I'm trying my best to go legit, but it will take time. I'm selling off my businesses. I'm running a legitimate windmill operation and making a good profit from the utility company."

Stevie stopped and turned to face his father. "You're going to give up your dope business? I don't believe you."

"I got a buyer for my meth operation. Son, I'm afraid you're not going to like who I'm selling it to."

"I don't care. I don't want to hear it."

"Okay, then, have it your way, but I've got a problem." Suddenly Sam became anxious.

"Judging from the look on your face, it must be a whopper."

"See that land across the road? That tract also belongs to Elizabeth. It's over a hundred wooded acres. I want to buy it."

Stevie laughed ironically. "Oh, so that's why you've taken up with Lizzie. You want her land, but correct me if I'm wrong, she doesn't own it. That's her husband's land. And if both of their names are on the deed, she can't sell it by herself."

"I know that," Sam thundered.

"I hate to tell ya this, but Lizzie will have to wait several years before she can legally declare her husband dead. Isn't that about five or seven or ten years?"

"That's about right," Sam shrugged.

"What if he's not dead and comes back? She'll have to divorce him, and guess what? I'm bankin' she gits nothing."

"I don't think that will happen."

Stevie continued without comment to his father's last remark, "This means you can't marry her. Wake up, Dad, the Howe land isn't fit for windmills. Doesn't the land have to be flat?"

Sam threw his cigar down and stepped on it. "A land development firm wants to buy it."

"What? Why?"

"Elizabeth's land is the only one around these parts that connect a state road to the interstate."

"You could have told me this crap on the phone."

"Dammit, I'm being investigated. I'm sure of it. I don't want anyone but my sons to know my business."

"Why should you care if Lizzie sells the land to this business? What's it to you?"

"Remember that Russian guy your dear old dad put on a plane back to New York?"

"Yeah? What of it?"

"He never made it."

Stevie leaned up against the Tundra and shook his head in doubt. "You murdered him?"

Sam put his hands in the air. "I didn't do it," he answered irritably. "One of my guys acted in self-defense."

"Yeah, right! Where'd you bury him?"

Sam shrugged his shoulders, looked away, and didn't answer.

Putting two-and-two together, Stevie asked, "Why did you bury the dude on Lizzie's land where the body could be found? Have you lost your mind?"

"That's my point. If Elizabeth sells to the land developers, they'll have their bulldozers dig up the area so they can build. If you remember, the Russian was killed in a snow storm. Wasn't exactly great weather to dig the grave. The body is buried close to where the prime development area is. I'm sure it'll be found. Then my ass is up a creek without a paddle."

"I don't know how the law would point it at you. Unless you left your business card in the guy's jacket. Come on, let's hurry this along. What is it you want from me?"

"I did you a service, now you need to do me a service."

"What are you talking about?"

"I got rid of the threat to your love interest, so help me with mine so I can get married."

"I know who you're referring to. Katherine Cokenberger is just a friend."

"You must think your dear old dad is stupid. You don't have much of a poker face, son."

"That's none of your business. What is it you want me to do?" Stevie asked a second time.

"There're other bodies buried there as well."

"I ain't a grave digger," Stevie said with disgust, pouring over his face.

"Forget the grave digging, there's something else I want you to do. I got rid of that low-life who was messing with my business —"

"Who are you talkin' about?"

"That big shot director who drives the Mercedes."

"You shot Dr. Goodwin? Geez, dad, why did you do it right in front of your girlfriend's property?"

"Because the idiot stopped his car there. I'd planned on doing it a little bit farther up the road."

"What was he to you?"

"He was our main source for angel dust —"

"PCP?" Stevie cut him off, and then asked incredulously, "So now you're dealing in meth and PCP?"

"Well, son, the opportunity came about when Dr. Goodwin moved into town. Your girlfriend hired him as the director of the animal shelter, but the salary didn't exactly pay for his lifestyle."

Stevie threw his father a dirty look. "Katherine Cokenberger hired him at the Animal Rescue Center. It's a no-kill shelter."

"Yeah, that's right. I understand he's a damn good vet, well, was. He came to me and said he had a means to get PCP, and that we'd be able to do a little business together. Doc needed money. I helped him out. It's simple. Supply and demand. Where do you think he got the money to buy his Mercedes?"

"I don't see how it's good for business to kill the guy who's your main supplier."

"He screwed up a deal. I won't bother you with the nitty-gritty, but here's my dilemma. A woman friend of mine in the sheriff's department told me there was a witness."

"A woman friend? Damn, Dad, how many women do you have?"

"Not sayin'. Just that there was a witness. She's as stupid as stupid can be. We've got to take her out before she changes her story to what really happened."

"What's she saying happened?"

"Here's the joke. She said Elizabeth cast a spell on a scarecrow and he shot Goodwin."

"That's ridiculous. Who are you talking about?"

"Melinda Hudson."

"What the hell was she doing out there?"

"She was having a fling with him."

"The scarecrow?"

"No, you idiot. Doc Goodwin. You need to shoot her before she brings the house down like a stack of cards."

"No one is going to believe her stupid story. Where was she when you shot him?"

"Parked in Bud Baxter's service lane."

"Did you see her?"

"No, and I really scanned the scene before I left."

"Then don't worry about it. Like I said, no one will believe her."

"She works at the diner. You can wait for her to get off work, then shoot her."

"I ain't a murderer," Stevie stormed. "I ain't doin' it! Case closed."

"You could make a great deal of money off of this land deal. I want to set you and Salina up for life, so she's got the best things in life."

"What?" Stevie shook his head in confusion. "In one minute you're discussing your son killing someone, then in the next, you're talkin' like a typical grandfather concerned about the welfare of his grandchild."

"That's it in a nutshell. Don't forget, son, Elizabeth's land is worth millions."

"You didn't just meet Lizzie on the internet. You set her up."

"No shit, Sherlock," Sam said, then changed gears. "Look, do this one thing for me and I'll never ask you to do anything else. Scout's honor."

"Yeah, that's because I'll get caught and be sent up for the rest of my life. I'm goin' now. I don't want to talk to you for a while. Just leave Salina and me alone."

"Are you sure this is what you really want to do?" Sam said, removing his phone from his suit jacket. "With one call, I can stop what's going to happen."

"What do you mean? Stop what from happenin'?" Stevie asked.

"You gotta understand, son, this is strictly business. With Dr. Goodwin out of the picture, I'm selling his last batch of PCP, and then I won't be in the angel dust business anymore. I've also got an interested buyer who wants the meth lab over by Chester's Snow Angel farm —"

"You mentioned the meth lab before. Who are you selling it to? Now I want to know."

Sam didn't answer, but looked irritated. He punched in a number and spoke into the phone. "Hey, sorry for my delay in getting back to you. Look, give me a few minutes. He hasn't said yes yet."

"Does No mean Yes to you?" Stevie asked bitterly, heading back to his truck.

Sam Sanders followed, and grabbed Stevie's door handle.

"Hey, let go," Stevie ordered.

His father's face took on a murderous expression. "I won't take no for an answer."

"Who are you talking to on the phone?" Stevie demanded in exasperation.

"That's none of your business, but in answer to your question: Your ex-wife's mother," Sam said, slowly enunciating each word, "is buying my meth business."

Stevie became highly upset. "Big Mama? Get your hands off the door," he exploded. Instantly, Stevie worried about Salina. "Where's Big Mama now?" he implored. His ex-wife's mother was a force to be reckoned with. She'd already said she'd take Salina away from him if he screwed up. So far, he hadn't screwed up, but he never trusted her to keep a promise.

Sam let go of the door, and answered with a question, "Why, son, I'm not sure why you're getting so overwrought?"

"Because *that* woman wants custody of Salina!"

"What? I didn't know."

"Where is she, dammit?"

"In Erie. She's staying at the Erie Hotel."

Stevie put his pickup in reverse, backed up, turned around and sped down the muddy gravel road. He hit a bump and nearly lost control of his truck. Speeding down the country road, he dug out his cell from his jeans' back pocket. Even though it was late, he called Salina's phone anyway. It rang five times, then went to voice mail. He panicked and drove even faster. He had to make sure his daughter was okay and not in the clutches of his evil ex-mother-in-law.

Rounding a bend, at a speed too fast for the gravel road, Stevie met an ongoing car full of teenagers. He recognized the older model Chevy Nova as one belonging to his younger half-brother's friends. He hoped Jerry wasn't in the car.

The glare of the car's headlights blinded him, so he swerved to avoid a head-on collision. He hit a deep mud puddle, and the truck started to skid. He struggled to stay on the road, but the truck veered to the right and glanced off a utility pole, then drove straight into a cornfield.

"Holy crap," Stevie cursed, terrified that he'd be badly injured and not be able to get to Salina. "Damn . . . damn . . . damn, not my new truck," he yelled. Gripping the steering wheel, in an attempt to stabilize the truck, Stevie jammed on the brakes, then he tapped them lightly to avoid a skid. The truck skidded anyway. The truck slid through the cornfield, hitting row after row of tall corn stalks that were nearly ready for harvest. The sound of the hardened corn husks hitting the truck was very loud. Stevie's worst fear was that he'd hit a dip in the field and flip the Ram over.

"Stop already," Stevie yelled at his truck. "What's taking you so long?" When the truck finally stopped,

Stevie quickly turned off the engine. Corn stalks were flammable. He didn't want the stalks underneath the chassis to catch on fire from the hot catalytic converter, hit the gas line, and blow up.

He exhaled a sigh of relief that the airbags didn't deploy. *Lucky me*, he thought.

He glanced around the cab, assessing the damage. The windshield was a mass of cracks and partially broken out by the hardened ears of corn. His driver's side window was knocked out.

Corn stalks had jammed through the window opening. He slowly opened his door, pushing the stalks out of the way. He stepped out of the truck and into the muddy field. His cowboy boots sank several inches into the mud. "Damn, not my new boots. Anything else gonna happen?" he asked ruefully.

He stepped around the pickup, looking for further damage. The right passenger door was caved in from where it hit the utility pole. He could also see numerous dents caused by the hard corn. When he pulled a corn plant out of his running board, he noticed the knuckles on his hands were bleeding. He touched his forehead. It was bleeding too. He reached up to wipe away the blood and said, "Just great! When will this bad luck stop?"

A teenager ran down the leveled corn row. "Stevie?" he asked, surprised. "Hey, bro, are you all right?"

"Jerry, what the hell are you doin' out this way — this time of night — on a school night? Were you drivin'?"

"No, ain't my car. My buddy, Joe was drivin'."

"Any one hurt?"

"No, why? You're the one that went off the road. Joe's piece of junk is fine. I ran back to see if you got hurt."

"Did ya know it was me?"

"No, man," Jerry said awkwardly, then changed the subject. "Your head's bleedin'."

Stevie took off his flannel shirt, balled it up, and held it against the wound. "Can you boys give me a lift home? Truck ain't goin' nowhere."

"Sure, follow me."

"I'll catch up with ya. Gotta lock my toolbox."

"Hate to tell ya this, but I think your truck is totaled."

"Yeah, but my tools are in the back. Can't risk them being stolen."

"Have it your way," Jerry said, heading back to his friends.

Stevie climbed in the back of the pickup and made a path through the corn stalks to check the toolbox. Before he locked it, he grabbed a flashlight, then he headed to the road.

Jerry was standing on the passenger side with the door open. "I need to make room for ya."

It was then that Stevie noticed the backseat was full of pentagrams crudely fashioned from wood twigs. "What the hell are these?"

"Oh, somethin'," Jerry said uneasily. "I'll explain later."

The driver yelled out, "Hurry up, man. Either get in or I'm takin' off."

"Give me a second, Joe," Jerry said, irritated. "This is my brother. And, ya better talk nice to him because he don't take shit from nobody."

Stevie gave Jerry a disapproving look. "Watch your mouth."

Joe said, "Sorry, didn't know. Take your time. I love being out here so you two can have a reunion."

The teenager on the front passenger seat rolled his window down and cackled nervously. He held a baseball bat against his shoulder.

Jerry swept the pentagrams to the side and climbed in the back seat.

Stevie said to the passenger, "Hey, Mr. Giggles, you git in the back seat. I ain't ridin' in the back."

Jerry piped in. "That's Chris."

"Please to meet you, Chris. Get in the back," Stevie said in a tough voice.

The teenager muttered something under his breath and complied.

Stevie got in. "Let's roll."

Joe put the Nova in gear and took off at a slow speed.

Stevie said, "Excuse me but you can do better than that. I've got to get home."

"What's the hurry?" Jerry asked.

"Salina might be in trouble."

Jerry yelled, "Step on it, Joe."

"No problemo," Joe said, speeding up.

"Not too fast. The sheriff is really workin' these parts since Doc Goodwin got shot."

"Me ain't stupid," Chris mouthed off.

Stevie said, "Salina told me some yahoos were vandalizing Lizzie Howe's property?"

"That ain't vandalizin'," Joe said.

"Tell that to the law when they catch ya," Stevie offered.

Jerry said, "We were just messin' with Dad."

"Messin' with Dad? I don't think you've caught on. Our dad doesn't do comedy."

"He's been datin' that woman. We've been puttin' that stuff on her gate because everybody in town says she's a witch."

Joe slapped his knee and laughed. "Ain't that funny?"

Stevie advised. "Joe, watch the road," and then "Like I said, the law is really watchin' that place, so don't put any more of those things back there. And give up smashing mailboxes. Trust me, you guys wouldn't have much fun in juvie."

"Where?" Chris asked stupidly.

"Juvenile detention."

"We'll stop," Jerry said.

Chris mumbled, "Like hell."

Chapter Twelve

Salina lay nestled under a summer-weight blanket with the covers drawn over her head. Moments before she was awakened by the sound of someone turning the key in the front door lock and walking in. The Foursquare was old and the floorboards creaked when someone walked over them. When the front door closed, she assumed it was her dad returning from his service call.

It was a school night, so she went to her room early, finished her homework, then put on her pajamas. At eight-thirty, she'd gone to bed and was reading a Nancy Drew novel when her dad popped his head in and said someone out in the country had lost power in the storm. He'd be gone for several hours and said for *her* not to worry. She'd smiled and commented that Wolfy Joe would take care of her, for *him* not to worry. He'd grinned and said he'd make sure the locks on the exterior doors were good and locked. She'd asked him to not close her bedroom door all the way, and to leave the hallway light on.

"Got it, baby cake," he'd winked. "See ya in the mornin'."

Salina startled when Wolfy Joe jumped on her back, frantically pawing the covers off.

"Quit it, punk," she said sleepily.

The gray cat growled deep in his throat.

"What's the matter?" she asked, sitting up and looking around the room.

Wolfy Joe sprang off the bed and crept slowly to the open bedroom door.

A woman's voice sounded from the first floor. She was talking to someone. "She's probably upstairs in bed."

Salina was alarmed when she recognized the voice. She climbed out of bed, walked to the door, and called out. "Big Mama? What are you doing here?"

Big Mama stood at the foot of the stairs. "Sweetie, come to grandma. I need to talk to you."

"Where's Dad?"

"That's what I need to talk to you about."

Salina stood motionless and refused to budge. She was very wise for her thirteen years. Having developed a keen sense of when something wasn't right, from the years she spent with her drug-abusing mother, she had no intention of going downstairs to her grandmother. "I want my Dad," she demanded.

"Darlin' girl," Big Mama said in a sugary, sweet voice. "Your Daddy found out I was in town, so he called to ask me to come over because you were here by yourself."

Salina moved to the staircase railing and leaned over. "No, he didn't," she sassed. "How did you get in? Who's with you?"

"I little less lip from you, Salina, would be appreciated. It's your Uncle Mike," the man said gruffly. "Do what Big Mama said. Get dressed and come down here."

Uncle Mike, Salina thought. *Mom's brother who hates cats.* She didn't like Uncle Mike at all. "Give me a minute to change. Okay?" she changed her tone of voice to one of cooperation.

"Hurry up. Don't make me have to come up there and git you," Uncle Mike threatened.

"Big Mama is tired. Do what he says, sweetie."

Salina bolted into her room, trailed by a very frightened cat. "Mir-whoa," Wolfy Joe cried.

"It's going to be okay," she said, patting his head.

She slipped on her house slippers and threw on her housecoat. Then she took her cell phone off the charger and thrust it into her pocket.

Wolfy Joe threw himself against her legs and looked up, eager for some kind of sign about what he was supposed to do. Salina whispered, "We're taking the back stairs to KC's house." Picking up the cat, she placed him over her shoulder. Wolfy collapsed against her, his body quivered. "Hang on. Be quiet . . . very quiet."

Lightly stepping down the back stairs, Salina was terrified to find the kitchen door standing wide open. She knew her dad hadn't left it that way. Something about the door standing open — at night — made her apprehensive. It was very dark in the kitchen. She wanted to switch on the overhead light so she could see but thought that would be a dead giveaway that she was fleeing out the back.

She tip-toed to the door, but the old floorboards squeaked with each step. Just when she was ready to walk out the door, Uncle Mike snatched her arm and dragged her back. Salina dropped Wolfy, and the frightened cat ran outside.

"Wolfy, come back," she cried.

Uncle Mike held on to her arm. Salina struggled. "Let me go. My cat. I've got to get my cat."

Big Mama shuffled into the kitchen. "Mike! Don't hurt her," she shouted.

Chapter Thirteen

Scout and Abra stood on the mansion's turret windowsill, gazing intently at the dark blue van parked in front of the Foursquare. Their ears swiveled from back to front, in an inquisitive motion. Scout's pupils dilated to large black dots, and she sprang down, followed by Abra. They arched their backs and began their death dance, swaying back and forth, hopping up and down. Scout shrieked, "Mir-waugh, waugh, waugh." Abra screeched in a shrill, high-pitched tone.

Jake was upstairs lying on the tall Renaissance bed. He was fully dressed. His plan was to take a short nap and get up at midnight to wait for Daryl, but he was so tired that as soon as his head hit the pillow, he was out like a light.

"What is it?" he asked, abruptly waking up. "What's wrong?"

"Mir-waugh, waugh, waugh," Scout cried again downstairs, this time at the foot of the stairs.

Jake slid off the bed, turned the overhead light on and keyed in the combination to the gun safe. Removing his Glock, he tucked it in the back of his jeans and dashed down the stairs three at a time until he landed in the atrium. Scout and Abra led him to the turret window.

Through an opening in the heavy velvet curtains, he could see an older woman and a younger man walking down the Foursquare steps. The man carried something. He couldn't see what it was. He spotted the blue van — a vehicle he hadn't seen before, and also noted that Stevie's truck was gone.

"This can't be good," he said to the Siamese.

"Ma-waugh," Scout agreed.

Jake opened the front door and ran outside. "Hey," he yelled in the direction of the Foursquare, at the couple heading to their van. "What are you doing?" Salina was struggling to be put down.

"Jake," Salina yelled. "Help me."

Jake pointed his Glock at the man carrying Salina. "Put her down," he commanded.

The man continued walking to the van.

"Who the hell are you?" the woman demanded.

"Put her down, now!" he shouted at the man.

The man totally ignored Jake's threat and continued carrying Salina to the van. Salina struggled and elbowed her uncle in the stomach.

"I'll break your neck for that," Uncle Mike yelled, losing his grip. He dropped Salina on the grass. She quickly got up and ran over to Jake.

With his free arm, Jake pulled her behind him. "Stay there," he whispered.

"Salina, get back here right now," the woman scolded.

Still aiming the Glock at the couple, "You've got two seconds to explain what's going on before I call the police."

"Mike, get in the van and wait for me."

Mike scowled, then moved toward the driver's side of the van.

Jake warned, "Hey, you Mike, get back here. Stand next to the woman."

Mike reluctantly obliged and walked back.

"I can explain," the woman said, starting to walk over to Jake.

"Stay where you are," he commanded.

She stopped. "I'm just reaching in my purse to get a document. Don't shoot me."

Jake didn't trust her. He was ready to shoot.

Salina tapped Jake on the back. "She's my grandma."

"What?" Jake asked, surprised.

"It's true," the woman said. "I'm Salina's grandmother. My name is Delores Culpepper." She brought out a piece of paper. "I have a written court order that states that if Salina's father dies, I have custody of my grandchild," she said.

Salina began to sob. "No, it's not true. My dad's not dead. She's lying."

Jake stated skeptically, "Stevie Sanders is not dead."

"Yes, he is. I received a call from his father that he's been in a fatal truck accident and died on way to the hospital. Here's the court document," she said, walking over.

Jake didn't believe her. He took the single piece of paper and tried to read it in the dim light of the outside yard light. The first thing he noticed was that the document didn't look anything like the official custody order Katherine and he had signed at the courthouse. There wasn't an embossed stamp of the state of Indiana on it, or a case number, or even a signature of a judge or clerk.

A beat-up Nova, driven by a teenager, sped up and parked behind the van. Stevie flew out of the passenger seat, with three rowdy teenagers getting out also.

"What's going on?" Stevie asked, still holding his flannel shirt over his wound.

Delores looked shocked. "What are you doing here? We thought you were dead."

"Do I look dead?" Stevie asked, wiping the blood from his forehead wound away from his eyes. "Big Mama, explain what you're doing here?"

Salina ran over to Stevie and hugged him. "Daddy, you're bleeding."

"I'm gonna be fine, baby cake. I had an accident but I'll live another day." Stevie stroked Salina's hair.

"They got in the house and tried to take me," she sobbed.

"You broke into my damn house?" Stevie yelled.

"The door was unlocked so we just went in."

"That's a damn lie. I'd never leave the door unlocked."

Big Mama gave a pinched-face look.

Stevie squeezed Salina's shoulders. "Let me talk to Big Mama. Please, go back into the house. I'll be there in a minute."

"I can't. Wolfy Joe got out."

Torn between the current situation and the unexpected trials of being a father, Stevie said, "Go look for him, but don't go outside the back yard."

"We'll help," Jerry said, bounding after his cousin. Joe went as well, but Chris stayed behind. In the excitement of opening the car doors, a pentagram made of twigs fell out and landed in the drainage ditch. Chris fumbled to retrieve it, and quickly threw it on the back seat. Jake noticed it instantly, but was too busy with other things to comment.

"Wolfy! Wolfy Joe," Salina called.

"Here, Kitty Kitty," Jerry said.

"He doesn't like to be called kitty," Salina corrected.

Jake tucked his Glock back into his jeans. "Stevie, she says she has a court order —"

"We'll talk about this another time," Big Mama said, attempting to yank the document out of Jake's hands. Jake handed it to Stevie.

"No, we won't," Stevie declared, indignantly.

"That document belongs to me," Big Mama protested. "Give it to me."

"Not anymore," Stevie answered, stuffing it in his pocket. "Now get off my property and don't come back. You'll never have custody of my daughter. You see this gentleman standing right there? Jake and his wife are the standby guardians for Salina if something happens to me."

"No need to get your feathers ruffled. We were just leaving," the woman said. She strode to the van. Mike opened the door for her and waited until she got in. He then got behind the wheel and peeled out, burning rubber as he sped up Lincoln Street.

Stevie said to Jake, "Hey, man, thanks. I'm sorry you had to be a party to this."

"My cats woke me up, or else Delores and Mike might have taken her. Stevie, you need a restraining order against them. That custody document she handed me is a fake. Show it to Chief London as soon as you can."

"I'll take that under advisement," Stevie said, not wanting to get the law involved.

Jake realized that Stevie was still holding a flannel shirt to his head. "You're pretty banged up. Want me to take you to the hospital?" he offered.

"No, I'm good. I'll patch it up myself as soon as I get in my house. Need to find my daughter first. Salina!" he called.

"What happened to you?" Jake inquired, concerned.

"I wrecked my truck. My insurance rate is going to triple."

"Who are those guys?" Jake asked, referring to the teenagers.

"My younger brother, Jerry, and his buddies. I nearly crashed into them. I veered to avoid a wreck and drove into a cornfield."

"That's not good."

"Gonna have to have my truck towed in the morning. Too late to take care of it tonight."

Salina came around the corner of the house with a worried look on her face. "I can't find him."

Jerry added, "Didn't see hide nor hair of the cat."

Stevie said, "Thanks for lookin'. You boys go home now. It's late."

The teenagers walked to the Nova and got in. Jerry stayed behind. He shuffled his feet and looked worried.

"What's goin' on?" Stevie asked.

"Can I talk to ya alone."

"Sure," Stevie said, walking over. "What's up?"

"Dad called and said that some crazy guy in a red truck had done somethin' to him, and asked that we try and run him off the road. I swear I didn't know it was you."

Stevie touched his half-brother on the shoulder. "Your secret is safe with me, but don't do everything Dad tells ya to do. Trust me. He ain't lookin' out for you. Go home now. Catch ya later."

Jerry joined his friends in the Nova, and they left, cranking up their music as they drove by.

"Dad, did you hear me, I can't find him," Salina whined in a defeated voice.

"Salina, there he is," Jake said, pointing at the middle turret window. Wolfy Joe was sitting on the sill, looking in at Scout and Abra, who stood up on their hind legs and dangled their front paws, doing their meerkat pose on the other side.

"Wolfy," Salina said, running to the pink mansion's front porch.

The gray cat cried, "Mir-whoa," and leaped into her arms.

"That's one problem solved," Stevie said, joining Salina on the porch. He put his arm around his daughter, and the two of them walked back to their house.

"Bye, Jake," Salina turned and said.

"Bye, Salina," Jake answered, returning to the mansion.

Scout and Abra met him at the door. They both stretched up to be held. Jake picked them up and kissed them on the forehead, then set them down. "You'll be with your mom and furry friends soon. Thanks for warning me about Salina. I think that calls for a treat!"

The Siamese became very boisterous and flew to the kitchen cabinet where the cat treats were stored.

Handing the rowdy cats their treats, Jake said, "That's it for now. Don't want you to get car sick."

He pulled out a chair and sat down. He called Katherine. She answered on the third ring. "Hi, it's me," he said.

"Where are you? Are you on the way?"

"No, I'm still waiting for Daryl. Did Colleen make it?"

"Yes, we've been playing catch-up and stuffing our faces with pizza. She just went up to bed. What about you? What have you been up to?"

"I had to stop a kidnapping," he said, then explained in some detail what had just transpired.

Katherine was shocked. "Delores must really want her granddaughter back or she wouldn't risk going to jail with a fraudulent court order. I know Chief London said she was a criminal, but I can't help but feel a bit sorry for her. She's lost her daughter, and now, maybe, she wants to reconnect with her granddaughter."

Jake said, "You have a big heart, Sweet Pea. But Delores didn't send any good grandmother vibes out to me. There's something hinky about her and her son."

"How could you tell in such a short amount of time?"

"By Salina's reaction. She was scared to death of them."

"Poor girl."

"Hey, listen, I hear a loud truck idling in front. It has to be Daryl. Gotta corral you know who."

"Have fun with that. See ya soon."

Chapter Fourteen

The next morning at the farmhouse, Katherine and Colleen got up from the kitchen table and carried their breakfast dishes to the sink, then took their coffee cups to the front porch. Katherine chose the swing and Colleen sat on a wicker chair.

"I'm surprised the cats didn't bless us at breakfast," Colleen said.

"They got me up at six, so I fed them. Now they're passed out on my bed."

"Does eating breakfast normally make them sleep like that?"

"They were up all night, exploring. Didn't you hear them?" Katherine asked, amazed.

Colleen shook her head, "No."

"Honestly, you didn't hear the dumbwaiter going up and down?"

"I thought Jake fixed it so the cats couldn't get in there."

"He oiled it, so it wouldn't make that awful noise anymore, but he didn't fix it. Scout pries the insert door off, and Abra pushes the button."

"What a duo! They really need their own reality TV show. What time did Jake bring the cats?"

"Around one or so. When he brought their carrier in, Scout was having a complete catfit. She sounded like someone was murdering her. Abra was very good; she didn't make a peep."

Colleen laughed. "Yes, I've heard Scout having a catfit before, but I was so tired. I slept like I was in a coma."

"I'm glad one of us got some sleep. I certainly didn't," Katherine yawned. "It's a beautiful morning," she said, switching to a positive topic.

"It's really nice out here. I think I could get used to living on a farm," Colleen mused. "Know any hot farmers?"

Katherine snickered. "Really? I thought you'd always be a city girl."

"With Daryl out of the picture, I guess I could always finish school in Manhattan."

"I'd be very sad if you moved back," Katherine said with a frown. "Colleen, when I talked to Daryl yesterday, he said he missed you. I think he's having second thoughts."

"I'm not chasing after him. He's the one who broke it off." Colleen grabbed her phone out of her pocket. "Here, let me show you the text he sent me."

"Oh, no, you don't have to do that. It's private."

"No, it's not. Daryl told Jake and Jake told you, so I might as well show you the original." Colleen scrolled down and found the message. She got up to show Katherine.

Katherine read it. "I agree it's very cold."

Colleen took the phone back and read it out loud. "We need to take a break from each other."

"Brutal," Katherine commiserated, then thought, *Jake said he suspected there was another woman, but I don't get that impression at all. Something else must be going on.*

Colleen gloomily returned to her chair and took a sip of her coffee. "I'm sorry, Katz. Let's talk about something else." Colleen looked to the west. "You know, the only thing that creeps me out about this farm is the outbuildings."

"Yeah, there's a bunch."

"Six," Colleen counted.

"Why would rundown sheds creep you out?"

"Well, because anyone could be hiding in them."

"Why would anyone want to hide in a shed?"

"All sorts of people might want to — maybe a criminal running from the law or even an ax-murderer."

"Ah, thanks. That comment totally freaked me out. Guess who's staying tonight as well?"

Colleen muttered, "I was going to anyway. Don't want to leave you out here with an ax-murderer." She tipped her head back and laughed.

Katherine rose from the swing and set her coffee cup on the wicker table. "Would you feel better if we checked out the sheds?"

"Sure, why not. Let's go for it."

The two friends walked down the steps and headed toward the first shed. The rickety door was already partially open.

"Well, what do you think, Carrot Top? Should I open it all the way."

"Are you packin'?"

Katherine smirked and asked a rhetorical question, "Why should I?" She grabbed the rusted handle and pulled. A terrified groundhog ran out, brushed her leg, and fled to the cornfield.

Colleen jumped. "The Saints preserve us. What kind of creature was that?"

"You're the one addicted to the *Animal Planet*. I can't be sure, but it looked like a groundhog."

"A well fed one. Are there any more of those creatures in there?"

Katherine stepped in and looked around. "No, we're safe. I'll leave the door ajar, so the poor critter can get back in."

"Onward to the next shed; we've got five more to go."

Katherine walked to four of the sheds, opened their doors, and found nothing of interest. Two of the sheds were completely empty, but the other two held a rusted collection of antique farm equipment. Walking to the last shed, closest to the cornfield, she noticed it was the only one locked.

"Maybe this is where the ax-murderer lives," Colleen teased.

Katherine didn't answer for a moment. She scrutinized the antique lock. "This is curious. This lockset is the same kind that's on the farmhouse's front and back doors."

Colleen replied in a cautious tone, "Why would the owner lock one shed and not the others?"

"Maybe this one contains something dangerous, like pesticides or scary farm implements."

"Scarier than the ones we just saw?"

"Hope not. Some of those pitch forks looked like props from a horror movie."

"If the lockset is the same as the one on your front door, maybe your key will unlock it."

"I left my key ring in the house." Katherine started to leave. "I'll go get it."

"No, wait. See that rock against the shed?"

"Yeah, and?"

"It's the only rock there. It doesn't fit in. I bet it's a fake."

"A fake rock?"

"I bet it's a hide-a-key," Colleen said, picking it up. "Shut the door! I'm right." She pulled the key out and handed it to Katherine.

Katherine turned the key over in her hand. "It looks the same." She inserted the antique key in the lock and opened the door. "Look, there's even electricity in here." She stepped in and tugged the overhead light's pull-chain.

Colleen stepped in beside her. "T'is a nightmare to behold."

"I've never seen so much junk in my life."

Three of the shed's interior walls were lined with shelves from the cracked concrete floor to the ceiling. Plastic bins contained small tools, nuts and bolts, nails, screws, and a host of machine parts. One large bin was marked "National Geographic 1953 to 1970." A stack of bricks was to the right of the door.

"At least the farmer put labels on things," Colleen said, tongue-in-cheek.

"I'm afraid to move for fear that I'll trip over something."

Colleen pointed behind the door. "Katz, why are those cages in here?"

Katherine stooped down and glanced at the identification tags. "They're from the Rescue Center."

"They look brand-new."

"They are."

"Why would they be locked up in here?"

"I don't know. I'll check into it. In the meantime, if you grab one and I get the other, we can load them in Sue-bee. I'll take them to the Center next time I go there."

"Okay, good idea. Are we done here?"

Katherine snickered. "Unless you want to hang out and catalog everything."

"Not happening. This place stinks."

"It's definitely got that old house basement smell."

Katherine stepped out, and Colleen followed.

"Hand me that fake rock?" Katherine asked, locking the door.

"Why?"

"I'm curious why a hide-a-key would be here. No one in their right mind would want any of that junk stored in there."

"You know what they say. One person's junk is another person's treasure."

Katherine and Colleen trudged to the Subaru and loaded the cages. Heading back to the house, Katherine asked, "Are you still creeped out by the out-buildings?"

"Sort of. If I lived here, I'd bulldoze them. They don't seem to serve any purpose."

"I'll go inside and make us a fresh pot of coffee."

Colleen sat down on the top step. "I'll wait here. I've got mud on my sneakers."

"Come to think of it, mine are a muddy mess also," Katherine said, sitting down, and taking off one of her shoes.

"T'is such a mess," Colleen complained. "That's what I hate about sneakers. The mud gets deep into the grooves. It's hard to get out."

The cats began pawing at the screen door and caterwauling. "Yowl," Iris shrieked. "Me-yowl," Lilac added. Crowie began climbing the screen.

"Get down," Katherine scolded, without looking at the door.

"Katz, turn around and look," she said, pointing at the front door. "It's bizarre. Your cats are lined up in a row. What does that mean?"

Katherine hobbled on one foot to the screen door. "Calm down. You act like you're starving to death."

"Ma-waugh," Scout disagreed.

"Give me a second. I'll be right in."

"Hiss," Abra spit.

"That wasn't very nice," Katherine admonished.

Katherine and Colleen were too busy looking in at the cats, to see the woman approaching. When the woman spoke, they both jumped.

"Oh, you scared me," Katherine said to Elizabeth Howe.

"I'm sorry," Lizzie Howe apologized. She was dressed in a red halter dress, wearing her signature flip flops. Her black cats gathered around her. She held an aluminum pie pan with a foil cover. "I baked it this morning. It's blueberry pound cake. It's from my late mother's recipe."

"Oh, how sweet," Katherine said, looking at the pie pan. "Would you care to join us?" she offered, pointing to a wicker chair. She then noticed Lizzie's feet were caked with mud.

"I think I better sit on the step," she said, sitting down next to Colleen.

Two of Lizzie's cats padded to the door and looked in at the felines. Inside, five of the cats hiked up their tails and scampered to another part of the house. Scout and Abra stood their ground.

Colleen got up and sat down on a wicker chair without speaking or saying hello to the visitor.

"I'm sorry I started out on the wrong foot the other day," Lizzie apologized. "I feel terrible about it. I wanted to bring you this cake as a peace offering."

"Thank you," Katherine said, accepting the cake.

Colleen mouthed several words to Katherine. "Don't eat it. It's poisoned."

Katherine pretended she didn't see her and hoped Lizzie didn't either.

Colleen cleared her throat, "Does it have poppy seeds in it?"

"Oh, heavens no, I never put poppy seeds in any of my recipes. The seeds get stuck in my teeth," Lizzie said, flashing her brilliant smile, then she admired, "You have beautiful Siamese."

"Thank you. You have beautiful black cats," Katherine said, then bit her tongue for saying black cats instead of cats.

"I suppose you've heard about the trouble in front of my property the other day."

Katherine said to herself, *Murder would have been a better word choice.* Instead, she answered, "We're shocked that Dr. Goodwin's life ended so tragically. Have you heard anything about the investigation?"

"I was hoping that you'd know something because you're such good friends with Chief London."

Katherine gave a quizzical look and shrugged. "Chief London isn't involved in this case."

Lizzie continued, "The day of the shooting, I spoke to Sheriff Johnson and told him everything I knew, which was not much. I was on my screened-in porch when I heard the shot. I couldn't get to the front gate soon enough to offer assistance."

"I knew Dr. Goodwin only in a professional context. I didn't know him personally. Some people said he had a prickly personality," Katherine said, trying to get Lizzie to open up on why she didn't care for him.

"Yes, he was a prick," Lizzie said, not mincing words. "When I volunteered at the new rescue center, he tried to kiss me. I smacked him, and quit."

"Is that why he made up the lie about the number of cats you have?"

"I don't think he was that creative. He was sleepin' with one of your volunteers."

"One of my volunteers," Katherine repeated. "Who?"

"Melinda Hudson. She's very manipulative. She probably put the bug in his ear."

Katherine wanted to ask more questions about Melinda, especially the part about her being involved with Dr. Goodwin, but instead, she asked, "Why would other people in town accuse you of hoarding cats?"

"I don't know and I don't care. I take in strays, hire a vet to fix them up, and try to place them in a loving home. If I can't do that, I send them on their way."

"I'm sorry, what does *on their way* mean?" Katherine inquired.

"I'm dear friends with Dr. Sonny. Have you met him?"

Katherine was taken aback. "Yes, he's my vet. My kids love him."

"Na-waugh," Scout cried through the screen.

Katherine put her hand to her mouth to suppress a laugh.

Lizzie asked, "Did one of your Siamese just say No?"

"Scout had her shots yesterday. She's not too keen on needles."

"Mine either," Lizzie said. "Dr. Sonny and I have known each other since elementary school. I adore him. We have an arrangement."

Colleen leaned forward on her chair, in sudden interest. "What kind of arrangement?" she asked nosily, finally joining the conversation.

Lizzie petted the two tortoiseshell cats and said, "I originally approached Dr. Sonny with my idea, but . . . I'm getting ahead of myself. I take stray cats to him. Trust me, out here in the country, you'd be surprised at the number of people who abandon their pets on my property. Dr. Sonny checks them over, gives them their shots, spays and neuters them, then if I can't find a home for them, I drive the cat or cats to a cat sanctuary north of here."

"Cat sanctuary? That's fascinating," Katherine said with interest.

"It's not only a sanctuary for feral cat colonies, but also has an adoption facility on site."

"What's the name of the organization?"

"Kitty Cache."

"I've heard of them, but I forget where they're located."

"They're close to the Indiana/Ohio border. But getting back to me, what I want to do, I mean to accomplish, is to turn my land into a cat sanctuary. I'd like to work with you on the project."

Katherine smiled ear-to-ear. "Let me think about it, but the prospect sounds wonderful."

"Good," Lizzie said, getting up. "Amara, take the girls home." The large black cat jumped off the porch, and the other cats fell in behind her.

Katherine said, in admiration, "I don't know how you do that. Sometimes I can get my cats to follow me, but when I do, I have to bribe them with lots of treats."

"Don't you know? I cast a spell on them."

Katherine's and Colleen's eyes grew big.

Lizzie laughed. "I was just kidding." She continued laughing, and walked down the steps to the path that led to the cornfield. The tall oriental shorthair, named Isadora, darted back to her former position in front of the screen door. She seemed hypnotized by Scout and Abra on the other side. She reached up with her long, slender paw and tugged the handle to the screen door; the door opened a few inches and the black cat slipped inside.

Katherine couldn't get to the door fast enough. "Oh, no," she cried, mentally counting the seconds before a feline Armageddon occurred.

Scout and Abra stood tall on their hind legs, gazing at the lanky cat that dared to enter their territory. With their tails wildly thumping the wood floor, Abra broke the stalemate. She leaned forward and licked Isadora on the nose.

Katherine lunged for the door, and opened it. Isadora backed out, then flew down the steps, racing across the yard, to join Lizzie and the other cats at the edge of the field.

Colleen stepped in the door and was oblivious to what had just transpired. Instead, she focused on the blueberry pound cake, that was still wrapped up on the outside patio table. "Katz, what are we going to do with the cake?" she asked.

"It looks delicious. I'll get some plates."

"You're not afraid it's tainted in any way?"

"Lizzie seems rather harmless —"

"So did Patricia Marston when she tried to poison me."

"Ah, good point. Let's not eat it, but the gesture was very kind. After what she told me about the cat sanctuary, I'm starting to warm up to her."

Colleen waved her hand in front of Katherine. "I think she's cast a spell on you," she said tartly. "Snap out of it!"

Iris trotted into the room and collapsed in front of Katherine. "Yowl," she cried in an "I'm starving" voice.

Imitating Lizzie, Katherine said, "Iris, show Scout and Abra to the kitchen."

Iris jumped up and did just that. Scout and Abra raced after her.

Katherine said, "See, I cast a spell on my cats."

"Pull the other one," Colleen said. "It's got bells on it."

Katherine took off her other shoe and walked behind the cats. She did a double take when she entered the kitchen. Her purse was lying on its side with the contents scattered about the room.

"Okay, which one of you outlaws did this?" she accused, annoyed.

Colleen stepped in, saw the mess, and snickered. "Maybe the cats think you should change bags."

"Ma-waugh," Scout cried, leaping to the Hoosier's zinc top counter. She pried the door open and found the treat container. Using two paws, she pulled it out. The lidded plastic bowl hit the counter, then fell to the floor. The other cats ran to it. Only Iris remained close to the purse.

Katherine handed a treat to each cat, then said to Iris, "Don't you want one, sweet girl?"

"Yowl," Iris answered, pawing the purse. She slipped her brown velvet paw into the side fold and clawed out a key.

Colleen stepped back. "Did you see that?"

Katherine nodded, leaned down and petted Iris. "Good girl. How did you know I wanted that key?"

"Yowl," Iris answered, reaching up to be held.

"Not now, Miss Siam. Mommy needs to do something." Katherine picked up the key and compared it to the one she had in her pocket. "They match," she said excitedly.

"Why are you so happy about it? I wouldn't want a duplicate of my front door key in a hide-a-key rock out by the shed. That's an invitation to the ax-murderer to come in."

"Will you stop?" Katherine asked, amused. "It's not a key to my front door. It's a duplicate of the shed key. When I first drove out here, I tried this key in the lock and found out it didn't work. Now I know why."

"But why would Iris call your attention to it?"

Katherine shook her head. "I don't have a clue. She's a cat. Who knows what's going through that pretty little head."

"Seriously? You make her out to be an ordinary housecat. Katz, your cats are beyond ordinary."

"This is true," Katherine agreed. "When Dr. Goodwin visited me, Iris stole something from his pocket. I couldn't tell what it was. After he left, Jake and I searched the wingback chair and didn't find anything. I think Iris took — I mean stole — his key."

"Why would Dr. Goodwin have a key to a shed at Bud Baxter's farmhouse? Doesn't make any sense."

"Yes, it does. Mr. Baxter must have called the Center about stray cats and Dr. Goodwin was working on trapping them."

"I haven't seen any outdoor cats, except Lizzie's that day I came out here with you."

Katherine tugged her phone from the back pocket of her khaki pants. "One quick phone call will solve this mystery."

Katherine called the Rescue Center. Harriet, the intake coordinator, answered.

"Hello, Harriet. This is Katz."

"Oh, how are you?" Harriet's voice boomed over the phone.

Colleen mouthed the words, "I can hear her."

"Can you check your files and see if Bud Baxter reported stray cats on his property?"

"Give me a second. Searching right now," Harriet said, then a few moments answered, "Yes, he did."

"Do you know who took the Havahart traps to Mr. Baxter?"

"Dr. Goodwin."

"Did he return with any cats?"

"No, as a matter-of-fact he didn't. How are you liken' it out there?"

"Just moved yesterday. We like it just fine. Thanks, Harriet. Oh, by the way, there aren't any stray cats here, so I'll bring the traps back as soon as I can."

"That would be great. Take care!" Harriet said, hanging up.

Katherine held her hand against her ear. "Wow, she was so loud."

"Wait a minute," Colleen said, confused. "This doesn't explain the duplicate key in the fake rock. Why didn't Dr. Goodwin just use that one? I mean, why did he have to have his own key?"

"I don't know, except both keys are staying with me until I can return them to Bud Baxter."

Iris crashed into her legs. Katherine picked her up and kissed her on the head. "Miss Siam, I'll have to find another toy for you. Mr. Baxter will want that key back."

Iris struggled to be put down, trotted over to the treat bowl, and tried to pry the lid off.

Katherine moved over and gave Iris a treat. The other cats immediately wanted more and were loudly asking.

"Okay! Okay! Inside voices, please," she said, handing them more.

Chapter Fifteen

Later that night, a loud clap of thunder jolted Katherine out of a deep sleep. A flash of lightning briefly illuminated the room from the west window, and another crack of thunder rumbled through the night. She sat up and leaned against the tall oak headboard. The room was pitch black. She patted the quilt for the cats. Finding none of them in bed with her, she called, "Scout? Abra?" Of her seven felines, she knew the Siamese sisters would be the first to come in and check out what she wanted. This night, however, she was wrong.

The bedroom door creaked on its aged hinges, and Iris trotted in with Dewey behind her. "Yowl," Iris cried nervously. "Mao," Dewey bellowed in his booming voice.

"No worries. It's another storm rolling through. Where are the other cats?" Katherine asked, not expecting an answer, but hoping her voice would summon the other felines to the room. Iris surprised her by jumping on the bed, standing on her hind legs, and biting her on the ear.

"Ouch, that hurt. Are you confessing to something, Fredo? Are you the one who opened the door and let the cats out?"

"Yowl," Iris cried, head-butting Katherine's arm.

"Move over and let me get up, so I can see where the other cats are." Katherine kissed Iris on the head, then climbed out of bed. She stepped into her flats and walked into the hallway. Switching on the light switch, she was surprised the light didn't come on. She moved to the next bedroom and toggled the switch. It didn't come on. When she tried the hallway light and it didn't come on, she got annoyed. *Great, the power's off,* she thought. *That's just what I need right now, is to grope my way downstairs and find the electric panel.*

Walking back into her bedroom, she removed the small flashlight off the lamp table. Switching it on, she was relieved that Iris and Dewey, on the bed, had been joined by Lilac, Abby and Crowie. They were busy burrowing underneath the quilt. "Thank you, my treasures," she cooed in a soft voice. "You stay in here for a little bit while I find Scout and Abra." She closed the door, then moved back into the hall.

Colleen opened her door and stepped out. She beamed her flashlight down the hall. "I thought I heard something downstairs. Did you?" she asked in a frightened voice.

"Scout and Abra are up to something. They've probably got an innocent mouse treed and knocked over something trying to get it. I'll go down and check it out."

"A mouse?" Colleen cowered.

"We're in a farmhouse. It's probably a field mouse that got in."

"Katz, I think we got hit by lightning. That's why the power's off."

"Hope not. I'll check on that too."

"Wait a second. You're not leaving me up here. I'm coming too." Colleen went back to her room and put on her robe. She returned with her cell phone. "Just in case," she said nervously.

They both startled when they heard a loud thud on the floor below.

"What was that?" Colleen asked, frightened.

"The noise came from the kitchen. I think it's the damn dumbwaiter cover. Come on, let's do some midnight cat-wrangling —" Katherine wasn't able to finish her sentence. The sound of angry Siamese had reached an ear-splitting level.

"Waugh . . . kill waugh," Scout shrieked.

Colleen said apprehensively, "That doesn't sound like a mouse hunt to me."

"It's not. I need my gun," Katherine said, running back to her bedroom. She quickly opened the door and retrieved her Glock from the top dresser drawer. The cats were startled when she flew into the room.

"It's going to be okay," she said, faking a calm voice. The Siamese didn't buy it, but remained silent until Iris growled.

Katherine rushed out of the room, closed the door, and then hurried down the stairs.

"Be careful," Colleen called from the top landing, now too scared to go down. She clutched the newel post.

Katherine beamed the flashlight down the hall toward the kitchen. She heard the refrigerator door open and close, then the loud distress shriek of cats attacking something or someone.

Gripping the Glock, she moved to the kitchen. The floorboards creaked noisily with every step. Entering the kitchen, she could see the back door was standing open. The emergency back-up light outside on the service pole was on, but it didn't cast any light into the room.

A flash of lightning lit up the kitchen. Katherine heard movement in the corner. She flashed her light in that direction. She heard the muffled scream of a man backed into the corner with two angry Siamese at his feet. He was dressed like a scarecrow. His face was covered with a burlap bag with holes cut out for his eyes and mouth. He wore denim overalls over a red plaid shirt with tufts of straw sticking out of the cuffs. It was the same scarecrow she'd nearly hit when she first brought Colleen out to the farm.

Katherine beamed the light on the scarecrow's face. "I've got a gun pointed at you. You move, I shoot."

A barely audible voice inside the hood said, "Get those freakin' cats away from me."

"Scout! Abra! Stop. Go upstairs," she commanded.

The Siamese ignored her. Instead, they continued growling and doing figure eights in front of the man, ready to attack him again.

"Cadabra!" she shouted, using Scout's stage name when the Siamese was a performer in a magician's show. It was the only word Katherine knew that got immediate results from Scout.

This time it didn't work.

Abra backed up, padded toward Katherine, then sat down. She extended her claws and began licking them. Scout stood her ground, then swiveled her ears toward the open door.

Katherine picked up on Scout's body language, and warned, "Don't you dare go out there."

Scout flicked her pencil-thin tail on the floor, thumpity-thump-thump, in intense feline concentration, then lunged out the door.

"Scout, no-no-no," Katherine yelled. "Abra stay!"

Abra cried a loud "raw" and fled out the door too.

Colleen came into the room, carrying a baseball bat. When she saw the intruder dressed in the scarecrow costume, she screamed.

"Colleen, I've got it under control. Put the bat down. I want you to do something for me. Go back down the hall and find the electric service panel on the wall. It's that gray box. Flip the main lever up."

"Are you going to be okay?" Colleen asked, her voice quivering. "What about that . . . that . . . creature over there?"

"If he's smart, he'll stay put, because a Glock doesn't have a safety, and my finger is itching to pull the trigger," Katherine lied. The last thing she wanted to do was to shoot, especially at an unarmed scarecrow with straw poking out of his sleeves.

Colleen left, found the electric panel and turned on the power. Returning to the kitchen, she flicked the light switch. The two naked bulbs of the overhead light fixture bathed the room in bright light.

When Katherine glanced over her shoulder to see what Colleen was doing, the scarecrow tried to escape. He moved a foot toward the back door; the straw in his sleeve made a dry, rustling sound.

Katherine wanted to fire a warning shot but didn't know the exact location of Scout and Abra. What if they came back in at the exact moment she fired a shot? What if she accidentally shot one of them?

Katherine shouted at the man, "Stop or I'll shoot. Trust me, I know how. Lie down on the floor on your stomach."

The man took several steps, then slowly got down on his hands and knees. He groaned, then laid down. He mumbled something inside his hood.

"What did you say?" Katherine asked.

He didn't answer.

"Put your hands behind your back," Katherine ordered, then to Colleen, "Put the bat down and grab Scout's cat leash off the chair. We'll tie him up with that."

"Let me do it. My brothers taught me how to tie a perfect knot," Colleen said, reaching for the leash.

Katherine gave her a quizzical look. "A perfect knot. What's up with that?"

Colleen caught the look. "My motto is 'be prepared.'" She leaned down to tie the scarecrow's hands but stopped.

"What's the matter?"

"He's got that straw sticking out. It's in the way."

Katherine moved to the man and shoved the gun in his back. "Sir, pull the straw out, and then put up your hands where Colleen can tie them."

The man began to tug the straw out of his sleeve until his bare hands showed. Colleen wrapped the leash around them, then tied the knot. She moved back to a safe distance, extracted her cell phone and dialed 911. "Hello, my name is Colleen Murphy. A scarecrow broke into my friend's house. Please send the sheriff as soon as possible. What's that? No, seriously a scarecrow. I'm not breaking the law!" Colleen said indignantly. "This isn't a prank call. I'm serious. Don't you want to know where we are? Hello? Hello?" Colleen asked angrily. "Katz, she hung up on me. Now, what are we going to do?"

Katherine shot Colleen a frustrated look. So far she hadn't been impressed by the sheriff's department. "Give it a few minutes, then I'll call it in, but I won't mention the intruder is in costume."

"Lookie there," Colleen said, pointing to the Hoosier's zinc-topped counter.

The foil cover over the blueberry pound cake had been removed, and a large slice had been cut out.

Katherine said, "In normal circumstances, I'd suspect Abby did this, but if she did get into it, the entire pound cake, pie tin and all, would be on the floor."

Returning her gaze to the prone man on the floor, she added, "Colleen, he looks very thin."

"So?" Colleen asked.

Katherine asked the scarecrow, "Are you hungry? Did you break in to find food? I thought I heard my refrigerator door open."

The scarecrow didn't answer.

Katherine said to Colleen, "We need to come up with a plan."

"Plan? Feed him a prime rib dinner?" Colleen answered incredulously, not understanding Katherine's intention.

"Colleen, I meant, we need to come up with a different plan . . . than me standing here . . . holding a gun on him."

"Let's lock him in this room, find the cats, and get the hell out of here. We'll drive to the sheriff's office, wherever that is, and report it then."

Katherine shook her head. "Not a good idea. Gimme a second to think," she paused, then after several seconds, added, "We'll lock him in the pantry. Go over and toggle that wood latch."

Colleen stepped over and opened the pantry door. She quickly began removing cans of food and snack items. When finished, she asked, "Now what?"

"You've gotta take the shelves out. Lift them up and pull them out. They're not nailed down."

"Got it." Colleen removed the painted wood shelves one at a time and leaned them against the corner.

Katherine said to the man, "I want you to get up on your knees and as slow as you can, crawl to the pantry."

The man murmured something unintelligible and refused to move.

"Borrowing a line from Stevie, Katherine said in a menacing tone. "I ain't askin' you a second time. Now!" She nudged the man in the back with her shoe.

The man quickly twisted his hands and untied Colleen's perfect knot. Scout's leash went flying across the room. He turned and punched Katherine's right ankle.

The force of impact made Katherine lose her balance and she fell to her knees. The Glock dropped out of her hands, landed, and slid down the sloped linoleum floor. It came to rest against the base of the sink cabinet. The man lunged for it and with one fluid scoop snatched the gun and ran outside with it.

Colleen retrieved the ball bat, then raced to the door.

"Stop, don't go out there," Katherine shouted, sitting up on the floor, rubbing her ankle. "A bat isn't going to protect you against a gun."

"I wasn't running *out* the door. I'm going to close and lock it in case that nut case comes back."

"No, leave it open. Maybe Scout and Abra will run back in. I don't think he wanted to harm us or he'd have shot us already."

Colleen said, "I'm not going out there to test your theory."

"We've got to find the cats."

"No way! That lunatic has your gun."

"I can't leave them out there." Katherine got up and limped to the door and began calling the Siamese. "Come here," she said. "Scout. Abra. Treat! Treat!"

The Siamese rounded the corner of the closest shed and trotted into the kitchen with a clowder of black cats trailing behind them. The two tortoiseshell felines were the last to scamper inside. Lizzie Howe, using a cane, hobbled in and collapsed on a kitchen chair. Her left cheek was bruised. Red welts were rising on her neck.

"For the love of Mary, what happened to you?" Colleen stammered, scared out of her wits.

Lizzie answered, "Lock the door."

Chapter Sixteen

Sheriff Johnson drove his cruiser to the front of the Animal Rescue Center, cut his lights, then walked to the building. Melinda Hudson met him at the door, and opened it.

"Evening," he said, walking in. The sound of cats meowing and dogs barking in the back of the Center were very loud.

Melinda said, "Thanks so much for meeting me here. I was afraid to come to your office."

"Well, at two o'clock in the morning, you'd have a hard time getting in. The public doors lock at nine. What is it you wanted to talk to me about?"

The dogs barked even louder. "Is there a quieter place we can talk?"

"Yes, follow me." Melinda showed the sheriff into the nearest room, switched on the light, and pointed to a chair.

"I'll stand. Is anyone else here?"

"No, just me," she answered warily. "Why do you ask?"

"It's two in the morning, a young gal like yourself, wouldn't be at her place of work —"

Melinda interrupted, "I'm a volunteer on the weekend. During the week, I work at the diner."

"Normally, I would wait until morning to talk to you, but I kind of have a hunch you've got something important to say to me."

Melinda nervously fidgeted with her bracelet, twisting it around her wrist. She looked up and caught the sheriff's eyes. "Do you have your gun?"

The sheriff eyed her suspiciously and started to reach for his service revolver. "Why do you ask, Ms. Hudson?"

"Because what I'm about to tell you will get me killed, sooner or later, so you might as well shoot me right now."

"Whatever it is, spit it out." He relaxed his hand, and leaned against a desk, facing the door.

Melinda began to cry. "I'm a horrible person and I don't deserve to live. I've spread vicious rumors at the diner about Lizzie Howe being a witch. Now everyone believes them," she sobbed.

"In my experience, most rumors start with a tiny grain of truth. *Is* she a witch?" the sheriff asked.

"Of course not. That day Tony, I mean Dr. Goodwin died, I made up the witch incantation."

"It was a pretty good one," the sheriff said kindly, attempting to get Melinda on track of what she seemed to really want to talk about.

"That morning I broke into Lizzie's house. She was home and caught me. Her cats chased me out. That's when I tripped over the barbed-wire fence and cut myself. Are you going to arrest me for this?"

"Lizzie didn't report it, so my hands are tied. Why did you break into her house?"

"I wanted something from her safe. My mother's ring."

"Breaking and entering is a crime. If Lizzie does get around to reporting it, you could be in a lot of trouble."

"I don't see it that way. I used to live there with Nicholas until she killed him."

"Is this what you want to talk to me about?"

"Oh, no, I didn't mean that. I don't know if she killed him or not. I just can't imagine why he'd leave. Leave her, yes, but not me. He loved me and I loved him."

"But, let me get this straight. You're divorced. Nicholas married Lizzie. I thought you'd found happiness with Doc Goodwin."

Melinda sobbed some more. "How did you know?"

"Oh, today's not my first day on the job. I've learned a few things about human nature over the years."

Melinda tried to laugh through her tears, then wiped them away with the back of her hand. "My late mom had this saying she'd tell me all the time. She'd say 'Don't beat around the bush.'"

"Sounds like your mom knew what she's talking about."

"The shooter was driving a metallic gray pickup," she blurted.

"I believe you told me this before."

"I didn't tell you the make and model."

"It's okay to tell me now."

"It was a Toyota Tundra. It looked brand spanking new."

"How did you see that truck when you were in your car parked in Bud Baxter's service lane?"

"I wasn't in my car. I was standing behind a row of corn. I was peeking out."

"What did you see?"

"Tony drove up in front of Lizzie's gate and stopped. Another vehicle drove up behind him and parked."

"Could you see who was in the second vehicle?"

"No, because Tony had his lights on and the glare made it difficult to see past his Mercedes. I didn't know why there was a second vehicle, so I stayed put."

"What happened then?"

"I heard Tony yelling at someone, telling them to go around. I heard someone walking on the gravel. It was a heavy footstep. It must have been the driver of the vehicle. I heard a gun blast. I saw Tony slump against the steering wheel. Oh, I can't . . . I can't," she cried.

"Can't do what?"

"I can't relive it again."

"Try, Melinda. It's very important for you to tell me what you saw."

Melinda calmed herself and took a deep breath. "The person who shot Tony got in his truck and drove off. That's when I saw him."

"Who are we talking about?" the sheriff clarified.

"The driver of the Tundra. I saw him," she whispered.

"Come again? I didn't hear you."

"It was Sam Sanders."

"Are you sure it was Sam Sanders? Earlier you told me it was a scarecrow."

"I'm spilling my guts out here. I'm not lying. There really was a man dressed up like a scarecrow, and Sam Sanders killed Tony."

"If I take your word that there was a scarecrow at the scene, did he shoot anyone?"

"No, he couldn't have because he was in the cornfield when I first saw him. He wasn't anywhere near the shooting."

"Let's backtrack. Why would Sam Sanders kill Dr. Goodwin?"

"I don't know," Melinda said. "Tony never mentioned Sam to me — ever. But I do know Sam murdered Tony."

"Just out of curiosity, how do you know Sam Sanders?"

"I had a fling with him about a year ago."

The sheriff gave a disapproving look.

Melinda saw the look. "Don't judge me," she said. "I've been lonely since Nicholas left me."

"I apologize. Melinda, this is big. Are you willing to testify in a court of law what you've told me?"

"Can't you shoot me now, so I don't have too?"

"Enough of that. Here's a question I'll throw out to you. Did Sam Sanders see you?"

She shook her head. "I don't think so. I was in the cornfield a few rows back. If he did, I'd be dead already."

"Have you told anyone else what you've told me, like your friends?"

"No, I thought I'd talk to you first."

"Where do you live?"

"I rent a room at the Erie Hotel."

"You're going to need some protection. I'll make a few calls, but you can't walk out that door."

"Why not?"

"Sam Sanders won't think twice about killing you."

Melinda buried her head in her hands. "I know," she cried.

"I've spent my entire career trying to nail this bastard, and you're my ticket to do that."

"Can't I text my aunt and let her know what's going on?"

"No, not right now. Sit tight." The sheriff pulled out his cell and began making calls. When finished, he said, "I've got a few law enforcement folks who want to talk to you."

"Tonight?" she asked.

"They'll be here in a few."

Chapter Seventeen

Colleen lunged to shut the kitchen back door but hesitated. An antique filigreed-brass key was in the exterior lockset. She pulled it out and slammed the door, then she inserted the key into the inside lock and turned it. "That's the last time that raggedy scarecrow is going to get in here. He left his blasted key!"

Katherine's eyes grew big. "He had a key!" she said, horrified. "I wonder who else does."

Lizzie moaned.

Katherine winced with pain and limped over to Lizzie. "Are you okay?"

"Let me catch my breath," Lizzie said, scanning the room for her cats.

Isadora stood tall next to Scout and Abra. Abra began washing the black cat's pointed ears. Amara stood back and eyed the Siamese with guarded interest. The kitten, Sabrina, ran to Katherine and climbed her pajamas until she was resting against Katherine's chest, purring loudly. "Ah, sweet girl," Katherine cooed, petting her.

"Come," Lizzie said, and the cats ambled over and sat down by her chair.

Katherine set Sabrina on the floor. The kitten scampered to the back of Lizzie's legs.

Katherine thought, *A scarecrow is running amok with my gun. A witch stumbles into my kitchen. She must have cast a spell on her cats, because they obey her every command. I'll make sure, when this nightmare is over, that I ask how she did it.*

Colleen stood cautiously by the back door, afraid the scarecrow would come back. With every bit of courage, she inched the curtain to one side. Peering out, she said, "Katz, I think the storm has moved on, but it's really dark out there. I can't see past the first shed."

Katherine hobbled to a chair and sat down, close to Lizzie.

Lizzie was visibly shaking. She wrung her hands. "I'm so sorry for barging in. Let me rest a minute and then I'll take my cats and leave."

"You can stay here as long as you like, but please tell us what's going on?" Katherine asked in a concerned voice.

Lizzie started to cry. The large black cat, Amara, leaped in her arms. Lizzie buried her face in her fur. "My life has been a living hell," she sobbed. "I'm scared to death the folks in Erie are going to burn me at the stake. I'm being stalked by this crazy man dressed in a scarecrow getup. I mean 'who does that'?"

"Have you told the sheriff?"

"Heavens no. I have to watch everything I say and do. People are accusing me of all sorts of awful things. Saying I'm a witch. Saying I'm a cat hoarder. I don't know who started these awful rumors." Lizzie reached into her pocket and pulled out a Kleenex. She dabbed her eyes.

Colleen noted. "This is the Twenty-First Century. People don't burn witches at the stake . . . I mean . . . I didn't mean to refer to you as a witch. Forget I said that," she blundered.

Katherine asked, alarmed. "Why are you walking with a cane?"

Lizzie didn't answer and continued sobbing. "I'm a complete idiot," she cried. "I've been so lonely these days. I signed up on a dating website and I met a man online. At first, he was so sweet to me. He sent me the most precious love letters. After a short while, I agreed to meet him. Turns out he's from this area. He was wonderful, brought me flowers, wined and dined me, then I found out he's not what I thought he was. He just wants to use me to get my land."

"If he's from this area, who is he?" Colleen asked.

Lizzie shook her head. "I can't . . . I can't say."

"Who wants your land?" Katherine prodded.

"I was with him this evening. I told him my plans for the cat sanctuary. He blew up and said I was a fool to want to use my husband's land for something so ridiculous. I blew up too and told him to get out. I said I'd never marry him, and that's when he beat me up."

"Lizzie, do you need to go to the hospital?"

Colleen offered, "I can call an ambulance," reaching in her pocket for her cell.

"No, thank you. It's not necessary. If anything was broken, I wouldn't have been able to come over here, but he threatened to kill me and my cats if I didn't cooperate."

"Cooperate? How?" Katherine urged.

"Behind my back, he contacted an attorney and found out that I can petition the court to get a death in absentia ruling to declare my husband legally dead. In Indiana, I don't have to wait seven years, like I thought. I can do it now."

"You don't have to do it."

"But that's where you're wrong. He said that if I didn't have Nicholas declared legally dead, and marry him, he'd murder me and my cats in our sleep!"

"He sounds like a monster," Katherine said, shocked.

"How could I have been so stupid and let this man into our lives?" Lizzie asked, choking with tears.

"Where is this man now?" Katherine said, terrified he'd drive up any minute and break into the house.

"I don't know. I got away from him and ran out of the cabin. He doesn't know about the path to your house. I'm sure he's probably searching down the road for me."

"You've got to report this to the sheriff," Katherine advised, adamantly.

"I can't."

"For heaven's sake. Why not?"

"Because this man is so powerful, if I don't do what he says, he'll kill me."

Colleen jumped in the conversation. "Katz, don't ask any more questions. This is way over our heads."

Katherine touched Lizzie on the arm. "Sweetie, calm down. You're safe here."

"I don't want any trouble. I want to live my life in peace and quiet with my cats."

Katherine nodded. "I'm afraid I have more bad news. Your scarecrow stalker has my gun."

Lizzie's face dropped in shock, but she didn't comment. She kissed Amara on the head. "Good girl," she said, then asked, "How can I go home now? I'm unarmed. I left my shotgun at home."

"Raw," Abra commiserated, trotting over and springing up to the kitchen table. She collapsed in front of Katherine, purring loudly. Katherine petted her on the head, then looked around the room. "Where's Scout?"

Colleen answered, "She booked it out of here a few minutes ago."

The three women heard two men talking in the next room.

"Who's that?" Lizzie asked.

"Dammit Scout," Katherine muttered.

Lizzie looked hurt. "Did I say something wrong?"

"No, I'm cursing one of my cats. She's an incorrigible lock picker." Katherine struggled out of her chair and limped into the hall. The door to the storage room was wide open. "Scout, get out of here. You're not supposed to be in here."

Katherine switched on the overhead light. Scout was standing on top of the reel-to-reel tape recorder. She muttered something in Siamese, stepped on the reverse button with one paw, and then stood on the play button with her other.

On the tape, a man's voice said, "I've been here for a month. If you're movin' to the City, how am I going to get supplies?"

An elderly voice answered, "I can't help you anymore. My wife is ill and I'm not so good myself. You have to go to the sheriff and tell him what you know."

"I'm not ready to do that. I want to make sure I have enough evidence to convict him. If I don't, I'll never be able to live here as a free man."

"I'm sorry to have to tell ya this, but a friend of mine and his wife are moving in to take care of the place for a few months. Once they move in, don't use your key anymore to get in the house. They're bound to see you, so you'll have to find another place to hide out."

The man sighed, then said, "Thank you, you've been very kind."

"Oh, there's something else. I called the folks down at the new rescue center. They're sending someone out to trap the feral cats around here. He said he'd need access to the shed in order to store some stuff."

"When's he coming?"

"This afternoon, so whatever belongs to you out there, you've gotta move it." The elderly man began to cough, then said, "I wish the best for ya. Just sorry I can't help ya anymore."

The tape fell silent for a few seconds, then Abra's voice came over loud and clear, from the first day Katherine brought the cats to the farmhouse. Scout pressed the off button and looked up at Katherine. She wore a eureka moment on her brown-masked face.

Katherine said to the Siamese, "Do you know who is talking on the tape?"

Scout gave an insane look, lifted up her hind leg and began washing her foot.

"I guess not," Katherine said.

Lizzie stood at the door, clutching the doorframe. Colleen stood beside her.

"If you wouldn't mind, could you play back the tape again?" Lizzie's voice trembled.

"Sure," Katherine said, moving to the tape recorder. "Scout, can you take your bath somewhere else?"

"Na-waugh," Scout sassed, slowing inching to the side. Abra leaped up and joined her on the table.

Katherine played the tape again.

Lizzie walked to the nearest chair. "My legs are weak. I need to sit down." Sitting in the chair, she began fanning her face with her hand.

"The suspense is killing me. Who's talking on the tape?" Katherine asked Lizzie.

Lizzie looked away and said, "Bud Baxter, and I can't be sure about the second voice."

Katherine thought, *She's lying. I know she knows who it is.*

A vehicle pulled up outside. Its tires crunched on the gravel drive.

"Who could that be?" Katherine asked, moving to the storage room's window.

Colleen was already looking outside. "Who do you know that drives a gray pickup?"

Lizzie jumped up so hard from her chair, it tipped over, hitting the wall. "We've got to leave . . . NOW!"

Katherine asked, "Is that the man who beat you up?"

"Yes." Lizzie moved to the door, and hobbled out.

"Where are you going?"

"I'm getting the hell out of here and you should too."

Katherine called after her. "I think it's a terrible idea to leave right now."

Lizzie didn't answer. She went to the kitchen, unlocked the back door and stepped out. In a tense voice, she said, "Amara, take the cats home." Amara meowed and trotted toward the path to the cornfield. The clowder of cats trailed behind her with Isadora bringing up the rear. Lizzie didn't follow the cats, but turned right on the sidewalk and headed toward the pickup.

Katherine raced to the door. "Get back in here," she demanded.

"This is my battle. Not yours. Lock the door."

Katherine stepped back, shut the door and locked it.

"Katz, call the sheriff," Colleen said, running into the room.

Katherine fished her phone out of her pajamas' pocket and punched in 911. When the operator asked the location of the emergency, Katherine hurriedly gave her the location, citing home invasion. "The intruder fled my house and is armed with my gun. Someone else we don't know has driven up the lane."

This time the 911 operator took the call seriously. She said, "Move to a safe area. Help is —"

Katherine cut her off. She rushed to the side window and sneaked a peek outside. The man had gotten out of his truck and was walking toward the rear sidewalk.

The utility pole with the overhead flood light provided enough light for Katherine to see he was wearing a ski mask and carried a handgun. "Oh, my god! Colleen, go upstairs and lock yourself in your room. Take Scout and Abra with you."

"No way. He'll have to break in here to harm us. We can protect ourselves. I've got the bat. Grab a butcher knife. I'm not leaving you alone with a madman."

"He's outside, and he's armed with a handgun. Our weapons are no match for what he's packin'."

"Where's Lizzie?"

"I can't believe this. She's walking up to him."

"Is she insane?"

"Now she's saying something to him."

Colleen rushed up to the window. "Move over so I can see."

The man grabbed Lizzie by her hair and thrust his gun in her back.

Colleen put her hand over her mouth to cover a scream.

The man pushed Lizzie to the back door and kicked it several times with his boot. "Let us in or I'll kill her," he shouted. "I know you're in there. She told me."

Scout and Abra trotted into the kitchen. The fur on their backs bristled to full height.

In one fluid movement, Katherine grabbed both of them and put them in the dumbwaiter. "When you get upstairs, hide."

"Waugh," Scout cried nervously.

"Please, for Mommy," Katherine said, her voice breaking.

Colleen snatched the insert door off the floor, placed it over the opening, then pushed the button. In her haste, she forgot to twist the turn-buttons to lock it. The dumbwaiter rose to the second floor and stopped.

The masked man kicked the door again. "Open the damn door or I'll blow her head off."

Lizzie pleaded, "Please do what he says."

Colleen begged, "Katz, don't open the door. He'll kill us."

"I'm sorry. I have to help her." She slowly opened the door. The man pushed Lizzie inside and forced her on a chair. He waved the pistol in Katherine's and Colleen's direction. "Don't try anything stupid, or I'll shoot. You, with the red hair, drop that bat."

Colleen reluctantly let go of the bat. It hit the floor with a loud thud, then rolled underneath the table.

"Put your hands up," he ordered.

Katherine and Colleen did as they were told.

Aiming the gun at Lizzie, the man looked around the room. He observed the pantry door open.

"Get in there," he ordered Colleen.

Colleen didn't protest and did what he asked.

He shut the door and latched it. Then he retrieved a large plastic zip-tie from his jacket's pocket. It was already fastened into a loop. Shifting the gun and aiming at Katherine, he walked back to Lizzie. "Get up and put your hands behind your back."

Lizzie slowly rose and turned around, "Please, don't hurt us. I beg of you. Don't hurt us."

245

"Shut up!" he yelled. With the experience of someone who had detained people before, the man used one hand to tighten the zip-tie. "Sit back down." He then extracted another zip-tie and secured her left leg to the chair. "Elizabeth, I'm not going to harm you, but if you breathe a word to the law about me, I will personally wring your neck. Understood?"

"Yes," she answered meekly.

He pulled out another zip-tie. Moving over to Katherine, he tied her hands in front. "Now you're going to take a little walk with me."

Colleen cried from the pantry, "No . . . no. Katz, don't go."

"Shut up," he said to Colleen. "I do the talking here. No one is going to get hurt. Do what I say and I'll be gone before you can bat an eye."

"What is it you want?" Katherine asked.

"The key."

"What key?"

"You know what key. Don't play games with me. Give it to me."

"I'm not playing games. I've got all sorts of keys."

"The one to the shed."

"Which shed?" she stalled.

"The only shed that has a lock. I know Bud Baxter gave you a key."

Katherine wanted to say that the retired farmer hadn't given her the key to the shed, but Iris had stolen it from Dr. Goodwin's pocket. She didn't want to quibble with an armed man. "I can't get the key out of my purse with my hands tied."

"Where's your purse?"

"On the floor by the refrigerator."

"Kick the purse over to me."

Katherine walked over and with a sweeping motion of her leg slid her purse to the man. "The key is by itself, in the fold on the side."

The man unceremoniously dumped the contents of the purse on the kitchen table. Finding the key, he said to Katherine, "Lead the way."

"Oh, don't go," Colleen begged from the pantry. "Katz, he'll kill you out there. Oh, please don't go."

"Colleen, I'm so sorry I let him in," Katherine whispered, then walked out.

"Don't try anything funny or I'll shoot," he said, sticking the gun in her back.

Approaching the last shed, the man ordered. "Go over there and lean against that fence post."

Katherine obliged. She thought back on the self-defense course she had taken while living in Manhattan. The instructor said to act helpless and scared. She didn't have to act helpless or scared, because she was already trembling from head to toe. She'd seen a video on how to get out of a zip-tie restraint, especially if it was positioned in the front. She had to wait for the best time to break loose, and prayed she wasn't harmed before then.

The man came up to her, took out another zip-tie and tied her leg to the post. Katherine thought, *Damn, the video didn't teach us how to get out of this one.* The man pulled the tie very tight. "Ouch," she cried.

He went to the shed, unlocked the door and walked inside. Searching for a light switch, he soon realized there wasn't a switch on the wall. "Where's the light switch?" he asked brusquely.

"It's a pull-chain. In the center," she answered.

When the man had his back to her, Katherine raised her arms up and using the muscles in her shoulder blades, slammed her arms down with such force that the zip-tie popped off. Then she leaned down and tried to undo the one on her leg. It wouldn't budge.

The man started throwing plastic storage boxes out of the shed. Katherine wondered what he was looking for. There was so much junk in there, it would take hours to sort through it. Finally, he walked out carrying his handgun in one hand and a small black case in the other. "Found it," he said jovially. "I'll be on my way now.

Sorry for your inconvenience. Someone is sure to come by in the morning and help you folks out."

Katherine held her breath and questioned what his next move would be. She winced thinking he was going to shoot her any second.

Instead the man turned and walked toward the farmhouse.

Katherine flinched when she saw the scarecrow approach the man from the side. He was pointing her Glock in the man's direction.

The scarecrow spoke in a firm manner, "Put your gun down or I'll shoot."

The other man answered sarcastically, "If I'd known I'd have to do battle with a scarecrow, I would have brought my flamethrower." He dropped the black case, but not his pistol.

The scarecrow fired the first shot. The bullet hit the man in his right arm, which made him involuntarily drop his weapon.

"Son-of-a-bitch! Are you crazy?" the man shouted, clasping his arm.

"Step away from the gun," the scarecrow ordered.

Still clutching his arm, the man stepped back two feet.

"Now take your ski mask off."

The man used his left arm to remove the mask.

Katherine caught her breath, and slowly exhaled. The man behind the mask was Sam Sanders.

The scarecrow reached up and removed his burlap hood. "Do I look familiar?"

Sam Sanders was taken aback but quickly recognized the man. "What are *you* doing back in town?"

"So I could be closer to you."

"I thought I told you to get out of Erie or I'd kill you."

"I did, but as the years went by, I decided to come back and nail you for what you've done."

"You've got nothing on me," Sam said cynically.

"Is that a fact? For starters, Dr. Goodwin was using this shed to store PCP. Then when the time was right, he sold the drug to you, and your people made it into angel dust. I think what's in that little black case will explain everything?"

Katherine was stunned. The director had stolen drugs right underneath her nose. *How could I have been so blind?* Suddenly she remembered the web page Jake had mentioned — the one with the Lladro angel advertised. The cats had surfed up the page. *Did they know the director was stealing PCP to make angel dust?*

"My lawyer will get me off on some technicality," Sam said confidently.

"Not when I tell the sheriff I saw you shoot Dr. Goodwin."

"Good luck with that. Who's going to believe you? All I see is a poor excuse of a man dressed up like a scarecrow."

"You might as well give it up! I know where you've buried your victims. It was pretty stupid of you to bury them on my land."

Sam threatened. "I still have those photos of you at the whorehouse to show your wife."

"You can't blackmail me anymore. I don't care if she sees them or not."

"You've got me then," Sam said, changing his tone. "Want to make a deal? Fifty percent of the cut?"

Colleen and Lizzie jogged down the sidewalk.

When Lizzie saw the scarecrow, she screamed, "Nicholas!" She fell to her knees, paralyzed by shock.

Colleen rushed to Katherine tied to the fence post. She held a pair of scissors in her hand.

"You're a sight for sore eyes," Katherine said gratefully. "How did you escape?"

Colleen cut the zip-tie on Katherine's leg, then whispered, "Scout came back down in the dumbwaiter and fiddled with the pantry latch. She busted me out and I freed Lizzie."

Katherine broke free from the fence post and limped around the fence. She grabbed Colleen's arm. "Get down. It's not over yet."

Nicholas was momentarily distracted by Lizzie. He hadn't noticed that Sam Sanders was stooping down for his handgun.

"Watch out!" Katherine yelled.

Nicholas looked back at Sam and warned, "Don't even think about it."

Sam reacted by picking up the black case. He threw it at Nicholas.

Nicholas fired another shot but it missed Sam.

Sam snatched his handgun and pointed it at Katherine. "I'll blow her head off if you don't drop your weapon."

An off-duty deputy from a neighboring county stepped out of the shadows. Deputy Daryl Cokenberger assumed a shooter's stance. He pointed his service revolver at Sam. "Put the weapon down. Now."

Sam continued pointing the gun at Katherine. His hand was shaking from the shock of being shot in his arm.

Daryl advised, "It doesn't have to end this way."

Katherine cringed and closed her eyes.

Colleen sat nearby and didn't move for fear Sam would shoot her as well.

Stevie peered around the corner of the shed. "Dad put the gun down. Think of your sons . . . your grandkids."

Sam turned and fired a shot at Daryl. The bullet missed and hit the window in the shed and shattered the glass.

Daryl retaliated and fired several shots. One of them hit Sam Sanders in the chest. Erie's notorious crime boss fell backward, dropped his gun and collapsed on the ground.

Daryl immediately pointed his gun at Nicholas. "Put your weapon down."

Nicholas released his grip on Katherine's Glock. It fell to the ground, bounced and landed in a mud puddle.

Stevie ran to his dad and knelt down beside him. He felt for a pulse, then looked up at Katherine and shook his head. He moved his hand over his father's eyelids and closed them.

Katherine broke the solemn moment, "Stevie, when your dad came into the house, he could have murdered all three of us, but he didn't."

"Did he hurt you?" Stevie asked.

"No, he didn't," she said with a sympathetic look.

Stevie quietly bowed his head.

Katherine said to Daryl. "Is Jake with you?"

Jake stepped around the shed and ran over to Katherine. "Katz, I'm right here. Are you okay?"

"Scared senseless, but other than that, I'm sure glad to see you."

"Daryl and I were a few miles from Erie when Stevie texted that Salina woke up screaming that something awful was happening to you at the farmhouse. He asked if we could swing by and pick them up to go check on you. Do Salina and you have some kind of psychic connection?"

Katherine shrugged. "Don't know. Where is she? She can't come out here and see this."

"She's in the house with the cats. Stevie told her to stay put and lock the door."

Katherine gave a sigh of relief.

Jake drew Katherine into an embrace. "My days of making promises to other people are over. I should have never let you stay here by yourself."

Katherine answered nervously, her heart racing a mile a minute, "I'd make a joke about being a pioneer, but my knees are knocking. I just want to go back to the farmhouse, change into something warm, and pour me a giant glass of wine."

Daryl hurried over to Colleen. "Are you injured?" he asked.

Colleen threw him a haughty look and refused to answer. She stormed toward the farmhouse. Daryl followed her and gently took her arm. "Colleen, listen, the sheriff is on his way —"

"You must be joking. A turtle would've been faster."

"I don't have much time to explain why I sent you that text. I was asked to be a part of a task force to bring Sam Sanders down. I was afraid the news would leak to Sam and he'd retaliate by harming you. I didn't want to take that chance."

Colleen's eyes narrowed. "Instead, you broke my heart. Why didn't you just tell me?"

"I took an oath to not tell anyone. When the sheriff gets here, I'll have to go with him."

"Why? You shot Sam Sanders in self-defense."

"I'll have some official explaining to do, which might take some time, so I want to apologize right now."

The sound of sirens grew louder as the sheriff and his deputies sped down the lane.

Daryl explained in a soft voice. "If I could take back that text I would, but I can't. I'm sorry. I just need you to know that I can't live in this world without you. I love you. I'd do anything to undo what I've done."

Colleen answered tartly, "A diamond ring 'round my finger would make a good start."

Daryl yanked her into a hug. He bent down and buried his face in her hair. "Will you marry me?"

"That's for me to know, and you to find out. Perhaps, I'll let you know on the Caribbean cruise we're taking."

"We're going on a cruise?" he asked with a wink.

"Yes, the one you book tomorrow. My semester is over in December. In the meantime," Colleen gestured with her ring finger, "I'll be needin' a ring."

"Making up is hard to do," Daryl chuckled.

"My sentiments exactly," Colleen smiled.

Nicholas walked over to Lizzie and helped her up. He wrapped his arms around her and drew her close. "What's troubling you, precious?" He smoothed her hair with his hand.

She laughed uneasily. "Oh, just about everything. How about you?"

He kissed her. "I've missed you."

Lizzie started to cry. "Nicholas, I was having an affair with Sam."

"I've done a few things I regret, so we're even. I'm here now," he said. "Nothing else matters."

The sheriff and two of his deputies ran toward the group, guns drawn. When they saw Deputy Cokenberger, they stood down.

Recognizing Stevie, the sheriff walked over to him. He looked down at Sam Sanders. "Is your father dead?"

Stevie stood up and nodded.

"I'm sorry for your loss."

"I ain't," Stevie said bitterly, walking away toward the farmhouse.

The sheriff quickly went into law enforcement mode. He said to the nearest deputy. "Get the yellow crime scene tape out of my trunk. Rope this area off," then he addressed the group. "I want statements from each and every one of you, including you, over there dressed up like a scarecrow."

Nicholas said, "Sheriff, don't you know me?"

The sheriff studied Nicholas' face. His mouth dropped. "Mr. Howe, my cold case just warmed up. Welcome back to the world."

"I need to tell you the criminal things Sam Sanders has been up to."

"Yes, we will get to that." The sheriff scanned the group and asked, "Which one of you is Katherine?"

"I am, Sir," Katherine said, limping over.

"You stated in your 911 call that someone broke into your home. Was it Sam Sanders?"

"Ah, actually not. I opened the door for him because he was holding a gun on Lizzie. But a scarecrow came in first."

The sheriff did not look amused. "That gentleman over there is dressed like a scarecrow. Did he break into your house?"

"I don't know if it was Nicholas or not."

"Why's that?"

"Because the scarecrow didn't break into the house. He used a key. I found him in my kitchen."

"What was he doing in your kitchen," the sheriff asked, getting impatient.

"I think he'd been eating a blueberry pound cake Lizzie had brought by earlier."

The sheriff wrinkled his forehead in confused wonder and changed his line of questioning, "Why are you limping?"

"It's nothing. I'm sure I'll have an ugly bruise. I don't want to press charges against Nicholas. The scarecrow who was in my kitchen wore a mask. I'm not convinced it was Nicholas."

"So there's more than one scarecrow running around in this neck of the woods?"

"I don't know," Katherine answered innocently. She left out the part about Nicholas taking her Glock, but that revelation would have landed him in jail, and she thought he'd been away from Lizzie long enough. Besides, there wasn't any evidence of Nicholas handling the Glock because any residual prints were now removed by the rain water in the mud puddle.

The sheriff said irritably, "That's okay by me. I've got enough on my plate right now."

Chapter Eighteen

Early October

Jake leaned against the zinc-topped Hoosier cabinet, drinking a mug of caramel-flavored coffee. Iris was hunched over her bowl, sending subliminal messages that she wanted a second helping. Dewey and Crowie joined her and licked the bowl just to make sure Iris hadn't missed anything. Lilac and Abby were perched on top of the Hoosier and sat with their backs together like a 1950s Siamese TV lamp. Scout and Abra sat in the dumbwaiter like relaxed grasshoppers and waited for their people to leave so they could take a ride to the second floor. Katherine scooted her cane bottom chair up to the farmer's table and opened her iPad. She began reading the online version of the *Erie Ledger*.

Since the death of Sam Sanders, the paper had been full of accounts of his life, his exploits, and his crimes. Upon his death, he owned a thousand acres of land, one tract belonging to his father and his father before him. Traditionally, the Sanders homestead was handed down to the oldest son. If there was a daughter in the family, she received nothing. Of the four sons, Dave was the oldest. He and his wife planned to build a house where the old Sanders farmhouse used to be. Dave also acquired the Dew Drop Inn tavern on the outskirts of Erie. He said he was thrilled to manage it. Stevie inherited the windmill operation and the land on which the meth lab had operated in an abandoned farmhouse. He was in the process of having the house bulldozed after the authorities had finished combing through it for evidence and the area was declared safe for human entry. Salina received a college trust fund set up by her grandfather before he had turned into a hardened criminal. Bobby and Jerry both agreed that they didn't want the remaining portion of the land, which amounted to three hundred and fifty acres of prime Indiana farmland. The estate attorney planned to put it on the market as soon as the estate closed. As a condition for the sale, Delores Culpepper (AKA Big Mama) could not buy it.

Learning that Sam was dead, Delores and Mike approached Stevie to buy the meth lab property. Stevie met them in their room at the Erie Hotel. Unknown to the mother and son, Chief London was standing outside the door, ready to come in and execute a warrant for their arrest. Earlier Stevie had met with the chief and showed him the fraudulent custody court order. The chief was eager to arrest them, but Stevie declined. He said it would be too much of an emotional toll on Salina to have her grandmother put in jail, especially since she had just lost her grandfather. Chief London reluctantly agreed, but did enter the room and read Delores the riot act. Soon after the chief and Stevie left, Delores and Mike quickly packed up their bags and fled to Kentucky. Stevie was relieved, and sure that he'd never hear from them again.

Sam's only daughter, Barbie, showed up for the funeral. Of all the children, she was the most upset, and was so distraught by the sight of the coffin, she had to be led away by her French boyfriend. She loved her father and tried to believe he wasn't a sociopath. In return for her devotion, her father left her two hundred thousand dollars, which she gladly accepted. Before the funeral and at the visitation, she was happy to see her old Erie friends. She was cordial to Jake and Katherine but had not asked once about Dewey and Crowie — the kittens she had given to them because her landlord threatened to evict her. Stevie stood stoically at the end of the receiving line, clutching Salina's hand. He choked up when he saw Katherine, then quickly recovered.

"Anything of interest?" Jake asked, finally breaking Katherine's reverie. He set his mug down, reached up and patted Abby on the paw.

"Chirp," Abby cried. Lilac me-yowled loudly, requesting the same.

"Okay, you too," he said, patting Lilac's paw also.

Katherine smiled. "The usual stuff. I don't know what this town is going to do for news once the Sam Sanders coverage dies down, but here's something of interest. Melinda Hudson posted an apology to Lizzie. It's short and sweet. Do you want to read it?"

"Not really. She should have never started the rumors in the first place."

"She blames it on an overactive imagination and the stress of everyday life."

"That's a pretty lame apology considering the fact she had the town up in arms to burn Lizzie at the stake. If I was Professor Howe, I'd sue her for slander."

"I guess it's better than nothing. As long as people read it, and realize the whole witch thing was a hoax."

"They've had a month to let it soak in. I wonder what Melinda is going to do now? I heard she quit the diner."

"She also quit volunteering at the Rescue Center. It seems she's taken up a new profession."

"What's that?" Jake walked over and put his hand on Katherine's shoulder.

"She's writing books. She's launched a digital novel, and Margie said it's selling like hotcakes."

"What's the name of it?"

"Book One of 'The Romantic Adventures of a Country Witch.'"

"You're kidding me, right? How do you know this information?"

"It states it right here in her apology. I'll read it to you. 'I wish to apologize to the town of Erie for my false accusations that Elizabeth Howe is a witch, cat hoarder, and murderer. I'm sorry I mislead so many people. Everything I said was the product of my overactive imagination. If you wish to read my new book . . . blah, blah, blah . . . you can order it online."

"She'll never change."

"You think?" Katherine said facetiously.

Jake shook his head. "She wrote off what she did to Lizzie like it was nothing, and then turned the apology into a sales pitch."

"She's a budding entrepreneur," Katherine said with a touch of sarcasm, then asked, "Something has been bugging me. It's about Nicholas. Why did he dress up like a scarecrow?"

"So he could move about the area without being recognized."

"But why a scarecrow?"

"Maybe the camouflage store was out of clothes that would fit him."

"Yes, he's so thin."

"That's because he had hardly anything to eat after the Baxters moved to the city. Well, Sweet Pea, that's all the news that fits. I have a class to teach. What are you doing today?"

"Oh, I thought I'd kick back my heels and do absolutely nothing but hang out with the cats."

"Sounds wonderful," he said, reaching down and kissing her on the cheek.

"Maybe I'll do this for part of the day because later this afternoon Colleen and Daryl are stopping by, and after five, Stevie is dropping off Salina for the weekend."

"Glad to see my cousin and Colleen back together. Is Salina bringing Wolfy Joe?"

"Of course," Katherine laughed. "They're joined at the hip."

"I'll bring pizza. Text me later with the number of pies."

"Deal!"

"Waugh," Scout seconded.

Jake belted out a loud Cokenberger laugh. "Scout, I won't forget the anchovies."

"Raw," Abra added with a yawn. Scout crossed her eyes and yawned too. Abra stretched over and pressed the UP arrow button on the dumbwaiter. The dumbwaiter rose slowly to the second floor. The Siamese sisters had earned a nap.

Dear Reader . . .

I love it when my readers write to me. If you'd like to email me about what you'd like to see in the next book, or just talk about your favorite scenes and characters, email me at: karenannegolden@gmail.com

Thank you so much for reading my book. I hope you enjoyed reading it as much as I did writing it. If you liked "*The Cats that Broke the Spell*," I would be so thankful if you'd help others enjoy this book, too, by recommending it to your friends, family, and book clubs, and/or by writing a positive review on Amazon and/or Goodreads.

I love to post pictures of my cats on my Facebook pages, and would enjoy learning about your pets, as well.

Follow me @
https://www.facebook.com/karenannegolden

Binge reading adds zero calories. The following pages describe my other books in the series. If you love mysteries with cats, don't miss these action-packed page turners.

Thanks again.

Karen

The Cats that Surfed the Web

Book One in *The Cats that . . .* Cozy Mystery series

If you haven't read the first book, *The Cats that Surfed the Web*, you can download the Kindle or paperback version on Amazon.

With over five-hundred Amazon positive reviews, "The Cats that Surfed the Web," is an action-packed, exhilarating read. When Katherine "Katz" Kendall, a career woman with cats, discovers she's the sole heir of a huge inheritance, she can't believe her good luck. She's okay with the conditions in the will: Move from New York City to the small town of Erie, Indiana, live in her great aunt's pink Victorian mansion, and take care of an Abyssinian cat. With her three Siamese cats and best friend Colleen riding shotgun, Katz leaves Manhattan to find a former housekeeper dead in the basement. There are people in the town who are furious that they didn't get the money. But who would be greedy enough to get rid of the rightful heir to take the money and run?

Four adventurous felines help Katz solve the crimes by mysteriously "searching" the Internet for clues. If you love cats, especially cozy cat mysteries, you'll enjoy this series.

The Cats that Chased the Storm

Book Two in *The Cats that . . .* Cozy Mystery series

It's early May in Erie, Indiana, and the weather has turned most foul. We find Katherine "Katz" Kendall, heiress to the Colfax fortune, living in a pink mansion, caring for her three Siamese and Abby the Abyssinian. Severe thunderstorms frighten the cats, but Scout is better than any weather app. A different storm is brewing, however, with a discovery that connects great-uncle William Colfax to the notorious gangster John Dillinger. Why is the Erie Historical Society so eager to get William's personal papers? Is the new man in Katherine's life a fortune hunter? Will Abra mysteriously reappear, and is Abby a magnet for danger?

A fast-paced whodunit, the second book in "The Cats that" series involves four extraordinary felines that help Katz unravel the mysteries in her life.

The Cats that Told a Fortune

Book Three in *The Cats that* . . . Cozy Mystery series

      In the land of corn mazes and covered bridge festivals, a serial killer is on the loose. Autumn in Erie, Indiana means cool days of intrigue and subterfuge. Katherine "Katz" Kendall settles into her late great aunt's Victorian mansion with her five cats. A Halloween party at the mansion turns out to be more than Katz planned for. Meanwhile, she's teaching her first computer training class, and a serial killer is murdering young women. Along the way, Katz and her cats uncover important clues to the identity of the killer, and find out about Erie's local crime family . . . the hard way.

The Cats that Played the Market

Book Four in *The Cats that* . . . Cozy Mystery series

    A blizzard blows into Indiana, bringing gifts, gala events, and a ghastly murder to heiress Katherine "Katz" Kendall. It's Katherine's birthday, and she gets more than she bargains for when someone evil from her past comes back to haunt her. After all hell breaks loose at the Erie Museum's opening, Katherine and her five cats unwittingly stumble upon clues that help solve a mystery. But has Scout lost her special abilities? Or will Katz find that another one of her amazing felines is a super-sleuth?

    With the cats providing clues, it's up to Katherine and her friends to piece together the murderous puzzle . . . before the town goes bust!

The Cats that Watched the Woods

Book Five in *The Cats that . . .* Cozy Mystery series

What have the extraordinary cats of millionaire Katherine "Katz" Kendall surfed up now? "Idyllic vacation cabin by a pond stocked with catfish." It's July in Erie, Indiana, and steamy weather fuels the tension between Katz and her fiancé, Jake. Katz rents the cabin for a private getaway, though Siamese cats, Scout and Abra, demand to go along. How does a peaceful, serene setting go south in such a hurry? Is the terrifying man in the woods real, or is he the legendary ghost of Peace Lake? It's up to Katz and her cats to piece together the mysterious puzzle. The fifth book in the popular "The Cats that . . . Cozy Mystery" series is a suspenseful, thrilling ride that will keep you on the edge of your seat.

The Cats that Stalked a Ghost

Book Six in *The Cats that . . .* Cozy Mystery series

If you love mysteries with cats, get ready for a thrilling, action-packed read that will keep you guessing until the very end. While Katherine and Jake are tying the knot at her pink mansion, a teen ghost has other plans, which shake their Erie, Indiana town to its core. How does a beautiful September wedding end in mistaken identity . . . and murder? What does an abandoned insane asylum have to do with a spirit that is haunting Katz? Colleen, a paranormal investigator at night and student by day, shows Katz how to communicate with ghosts. An arsonist is torching historic properties. Will the mansion be his next target? Ex-con Stevie Sanders and the Siamese play their own stalking games, but for different reasons. It's up to Katz and her extraordinary felines to solve two mysteries: one hot, one cold. Seal-point Scout wants a new adventure fix, and litter-mate Abra fetches a major clue that puts an arsonist behind bars.

The Cats that Stole a Million

Book Seven in *The Cats that . . .* Cozy Mystery series

Millionaire Katherine, aka Katz, husband Jake and their seven cats return to the pink mansion after the explosion wreaked havoc several months earlier. Now the house has been restored, will it continue to be a murder magnet? Erie, Indiana is crime-free for the first time since heiress Katherine, aka Katz, and her cats moved into town. Everyone is at peace until domestic harmony is disrupted by an uninvited visitor from Brooklyn. Why is Katz's friend being tracked by a NYC mob? Meanwhile, ex-con Stevie Sanders wants to go clean, but ties to dear old Dad (Erie's notorious crime boss) keep pulling him back. Murder, lies, and a million-dollar theft have Katz and her seven extraordinary cats working on borrowed time to unravel a mystery.

Acknowledgements

I wish to thank my husband, Jeff Dible, who took time out from his busy law practice to painstakingly edit the first draft of this book.

Thank you so much, Rob. You did an incredible cover.

Hugs to Ramona Kekstadt (and her dog Louie) for beta reading my book. Ramona has been my beta reader since "The Cats that Told a Fortune."

Thanks to my loyal readers, my family, and friends.

The Cats that . . . Cozy Mystery series would never be without the input from my furry friends. My husband and I have many cats, ranging in ages from four to thirteen-years-old.

The year 2016 was a tough one for me. My sister, Linda Golden, also known as author Alexa Grace, died from a rare form of thymus cancer. She fought a courageous battle. She was truly amazing. Rest in peace, my beautiful sister. You inspired me to become a writer and you lovingly pushed me to self-publish.